3000 80002
St. Louis Community College

P9-APU-026

FV

 St. Louis Community College

Forest Park
Florissant Valley
Meramec

Instructional Resources
St. Louis, Missouri

THEY SHOWED THE WAY

THEY
SHOWED
THE WAY

Forty American Negro Leaders

By Charlemae Hill Rollins

Thomas Y. Crowell New York

I wish to express my deepest thanks to Margaret Taylor Burroughs and Margaret Thomsen Raymond for their valuable assistance in the research and editing of this material, and to Josephine Glover Sanders, who patiently typed the many versions of it.

Charlemae Hill Rollins

Copyright © 1964 by Charlemae Hill Rollins
All rights reserved. No part of this book may
be reproduced in any form, except by a reviewer,
without the permission of the publisher
Designed by Albert Burkhardt
Manufactured in the United States of America
Published in Canada
by Fitzhenry & Whiteside Limited, Toronto
Library of Congress Catalog Card No. 64-20692
ISBN 0-690-81612-X

12 13 14 15

CONTENTS

Contents

Contents

ROBERT SENGSTACKE ABBOTT

1870–1940

Newspaper Publisher

Robert Sengstacke Abbott was born November 24, 1870, on St. Simon's Island off the coast of Georgia. He spent his early childhood in Savannah and went to school at Beach Institute there. Later he attended Claflin Institute at Orangeburg, South Carolina, and from there he went to Hampton Institute in Virginia, where he was graduated as a "thorough master of the trade of printing."

It was while he was an apprentice printer of the *Savannah News* that he came to love the world of journalism. Abbott knew that opportunities for advancement with the newspapers were limited for Negroes in the south, but he stayed in Savannah until he felt that he

1

had learned all he could there. Then he moved to Chicago. He had thought during his apprentice years that Chicago was almost a "Promised Land" for journalists, but when he applied for a job on the well-established papers—any job at all—he found that there were no openings for a Negro. One paper after another refused even to interview him.

He tried to join a printers' union, and was refused real membership, but was given a card which permitted him to work in a union shop. After working one day he was dropped from the payroll. He sought work in other shops, with the same result. Sometimes he remained three or four days in one place, but dismissal always came before he had worked a week.

After more than a year of this kind of treatment, he realized he could never earn enough to support himself by his trade. He took another job and went to Kent College of Law at night. After he received his degree he practiced law in Chicago, and in Gary, Indiana—but only for a short while. His first love was journalism, and in 1905, nine years after he had come to Chicago, he decided to start his own newspaper.

A friend, Mrs. Henrietta P. Lee, allowed him to use her basement as an office. He had one chair, a desk, and twenty-five cents in his pocket. Mrs. Lee's daughter, Genevieve, ran errands for him and took messages over her mother's telephone. Her brother, Benote, often loaned him money to help pay for supplies.

The first issue of his paper, the *Chicago Defender*, dated May 5, 1905, consisted of three hundred copies. Abbott wrote the news, solicited advertisements, printed the paper, and then peddled it to his friends. Three of his friends each took a year's subscription, which cost $1.00. These three dollars helped to defray the paper and printing costs—$13.75—of the first issue.

The *Chicago Defender* grew out of a great need, and from the very beginning it was a success. Its standard of news coverage was high, and its editorial policies extended far beyond the interests of the Negro community. The rights and responsibilities of all Americans became the hallmark of Abbott's editorial policy—a policy that has continued through the years.

The *Chicago Defender* has grown from a weekly to a daily newspaper, and is on sale at newsstands in cities and towns all over the United States. It has a daily circulation of more than 28,000, and more than 38,000 for the Sunday edition, which is circulated in eight foreign countries.

In 1918 Abbott married Helen Thornton Morrison, a widow. They were later divorced, and he married another widow, Edna Brown Dennison. He had no children of his own, but he was devoted to his nephew, John Sengstacke, to whom he left the *Chicago Defender*. Mr. Sengstacke is the present editor and publisher of the paper.

Robert Abbott received many honors during his lifetime. He was appointed a member of the Illinois Race Relations Commission by Governor Frank Lowden in 1919; he was president of the Hampton Institute Alumni Association; his fraternity, Kappa Alpha Psi, gave him its Laurel Wreath for Distinguished Service; he received honorary degrees from Morris Brown University in Georgia, and Wilberforce University in Ohio.

Abbott was a member of the Episcopal Church and contributed generously not only to his own church but to many other churches and charitable organizations, both Negro and white.

The Robert S. Abbott Memorial Award is given by the *Chicago Defender* each year to a person who has made a distinguished contribution to the cause of better race relations in the United States. A Robert S. Abbott scholarship has been established at Lincoln University in Missouri, and is given each year to a worthy student in the School of Journalism. The U.S. Maritime Commission named a Liberty ship the *Robert S. Abbott* in April, 1944, and a large elementary school in Chicago carries his name, a name that is synonymous with editorial forthrightness and integrity.

IRA FREDERICK ALDRIDGE

1807–1867

Shakespearean Actor

I RA FREDERICK ALDRIDGE, destined to become one of the great actors of tragedy in the Europe of his time, was born of humble Negro parents in New York City in 1807. It is not known whether his mother was freeborn, or a slave from North Carolina who had escaped or bought her freedom. His father, the Reverend Daniel Aldridge, was "a strict member of old Zion Church" in New York, and may have been born there, too.

Ira Aldridge attended the African Free School in New York, one of seven schools organized about 1787 by the Manumission Society for the education of freeborn Negro children. He was a bright, eager student who won the admiration of his Scottish schoolmaster, Charles

Andrews, and he was popular among his schoolmates. He studied at the school until he was sixteen. But then his mother died, and his father married again, and, probably because his father was a strict disciplinarian, Ira left home.

At that time most New York theaters posted signs announcing "Dogs and Negroes Forbidden!" The Park Theater, fronting on City Hall Park, however, had a gallery set aside for Negroes. What plays might the boy Ira have seen there? In 1818, James William Wallack, an English actor, opened in *Macbeth*, and played many of the Shakespearean tragedy parts Aldridge was later to play. His brother, Henry Wallack, came in 1819 to play in *Rob Roy*, based on Scott's novel; this was another role Aldridge was to make famous. The Wallack brothers were builders of theaters as well as actors and producers, and Ira Aldridge knew them well in later life.

The boy Ira might also have seen Junius Brutus Booth in *Richard III* in 1821. Booth later did many of the Shakespearean tragedies. He was the founder of the famous acting family. His sons were Edwin Booth and John Wilkes Booth, the actor who shot Abraham Lincoln.

The great English actor, Edmund Kean, came to New York in 1820, opening in *Richard II*, and also playing

Othello, Hamlet, King Lear, and *Shylock,* all parts that Ira Aldridge was to perform later.

About 1820, the free Negroes started their own "African Theatre," also known as "Brown's" for its proprietor. Here Aldridge gave his first performance, so far as is known, appearing in the part of Rolla in the play *Pizarro*—a part most sympathetic because of the passionate and patriotic speeches of the Peruvian Inca defending his people against the invading Spaniards. He was associated in this play with James Hewlett, a noted mulatto actor, who had appeared at the London Coberg Theatre, now known as "The Old Vic."

Ira Aldridge is believed to have delivered costumes to the Wallack brothers, and in 1824 he shipped as a steward on a vessel that was taking James Wallack back to England for an engagement there. Somehow he made the acquaintance of the English actor, who hired him as a "dresser" and for minor roles in his company.

There is some basis to the statement by Aldridge that he attended Glasgow University shortly after his arrival in 1825, and that he studied under a classical scholar, Professor Sanford, who was indeed a member of the faculty at that time. The university has no record of his enrollment, but this is not strange, for many students took courses without formal enrollment.

Aldridge came down from Glasgow to London, where

in 1825 he appeared in the melodrama *The Revolt of Surinam, or A Slave's Revenge,* based on the life of a tragic Negro hero, Oroonoko. This part had been popular among the great English actors for one hundred and fifty years, though it is too stilted for our tastes. A handbill preserved in the British Museum announces the first-night appearance of a "Tragedian of Colour, from the African Theatre, New York."

Shortly thereafter, Aldridge became known as "the African Roscius," after Quintus Roscius Gallus, a slave who made himself famous as an actor in ancient Rome. Between 1825 and 1833, he established himself in the English theater. He toured the provinces and the large cities of the British Isles, before appearing in the most famous London house, the Theatre Royal at Covent Garden. The press tried to prevent his appearance by every kind of name-calling imaginable. He was even accused of thievery while in the employ of the Wallacks. It was not until April of 1833 that he opened at the Theatre Royal in *Othello,* and "those two days in the history of the world, theatre and human progress will forever be red-letter days. A lone Negro of an enslaved people challenged the white actors in their favorite theatre in one of the greatest tragic roles Shakespeare had written."

It was one hundred years later before another American Negro, Paul Robeson, was to make as great a success at the Theatre Royal in Drury Lane, in the same part of *Othello*.

Aldridge now turned his face toward Europe, where he toured the Continent, playing not only *Othello*, but *Rob Roy*, *King Lear*, and a revised version of the horror story of *Titus Andronicus*, written especially for him. He gave command performances for the Emperors of Germany and Austria, and the crowned heads of Sweden and Russia. Honors, medals, orders were showered upon him, but he was particularly proud of one of his first medals, presented by the government of the Republic of Haiti, honoring "The first man of colour in the Theatre." Aldridge had played the role of Christophe, the liberator of Haiti, in *The Death of Christophe*.

His successes were recorded in the diaries, memoirs, and letters of the leading men and women of his time: Richard Wagner, the composer; Helen Modjeska, the famous actress; Count and Countess Tolstoy; the Russian poet Shevchenko, and Alexandre Dumas. One of his friends was Jenny Lind, the "Swedish Nightingale"; another was Hans Christian Andersen, who was inspired to write his only successful play, *The Mulatto*, after seeing Aldridge perform.

Aldridge was married twice. His first wife, Margaret,

was an Englishwoman. They had one son, Ira Frederick. His second wife was a Swedish opera singer, Amanda Paulina, whom he married after the death of his first wife in 1858. Three children were born to them: Ira Daniel, Ira Luranah, and Amanda Ira. All of his children were successful in the theater, particularly as vocalists. His daughter Amanda, still living in 1958, was a famous teacher of voice. One of her pupils was Paul Robeson.

Ira Frederick Aldridge, frequently in ill health from a lung infection, died in Lodz, Poland, on August 7, 1867. He is buried under a handsome cross erected in 1890, and his grave is still cared for by the Society of Polish Artists of Film and Theatre. He would probably have been proudest of a memorial to his honor in the New Memorial Theatre at Stratford-upon-Avon, dedicated in 1932, on April 23, the birthday of William Shakespeare.

A seat in that theater bears a bronze plate with the simple inscription IRA ALDRIDGE. It is one of thirty-three such chairs dedicated to the great actors in world drama: Burbage of Shakespeare's own time; Garrick, Mrs. Siddons, the Kembles, Kean, Forrest, Irving, Ellen Terry— and this son of humble Negro Americans is one of them!

RICHARD ALLEN

1760–1831

First Negro Bishop in the United States

Richard Allen was born a slave on a plantation near Philadelphia in 1760. He was sold while still a child to a planter in Delaware. Even as a small boy he felt a desire to preach. As he grew up his master became more and more impressed with the genuineness of his piety, and gave him permission to conduct prayer service for the slaves. When he was later allowed to preach to the family in the "big house," his master was converted by Richard's preaching.

The master realized the evil of slavery, and allowed all his slaves who chose to buy their freedom. Richard Allen and his brother worked hard for their master, and saved two thousand dollars. In 1777 they were freed.

Recognizing the unusual talents of this newly freed

slave, several church leaders allowed him to travel about the country with them on their circuits. He preached to white and black alike. When he preached at St. George Church in Philadelphia he attracted such crowds of Negroes that the authorities of the church proposed to segregate the worship. Allen refused to accept segregated seating in the "House of God." But the conflict persisted, and one Sunday white members of the congregation pulled praying Negroes to their feet and ordered them to the gallery of the church. Rather than accept this insult, the Negroes withdrew from the church. Allen immediately organized the Independent Free African Society, which later became the African Methodist Episcopal Church.

In 1793 a fearful epidemic of yellow fever attacked Philadelphia. People fled as the epidemic spread. Several of the city's physicians died, and nurses, too, succumbed to the disease. The survivors were exhausted by the work of caring for the sick. Hardly anyone was willing to visit the sick, and none would go near the dead.

In September, when the disease was at its height, the Negro citizens of the city were asked to come forward to attend the sick and bury the dead—at that time Negroes were thought to be immune to yellow fever.

At first the Negroes were stunned by this request.

They went to the leaders of their community for advice. The leaders were naturally the ministers of the two largest churches—Richard Allen of the Methodist Church, and Absalom Jones, who later became rector of St. Thomas's African Episcopal Church. These men "thought prayerfully about the situation," about the danger to their own people and about the tragedy that was overtaking the city, and finally decided that it was their duty to help their fellow men.

In the weeks that followed, the Negroes of Philadelphia, led by Allen and Jones, were constantly on call to help save the lives of hundreds of yellow-fever victims, and to bury the dead.

When the epidemic was finally checked, their efforts were criticized. A white citizen, Matthew Carey, published A *short account of the Malignant Fever*, which charged that the Negroes should have done much more than they did, and also that they overcharged the stricken.

Allen and Jones immediately issued a pamphlet, A *Narrative of the Proceedings of the Black People, during the Late Awful Calamity in Philadelphia*, refuting the charges. They gave details of the entire undertaking; and a statement of the expenditures, including receipts that they had received, some of which showed that there was not enough cash to pay for coffins or labor of burying. They had buried hundreds of strangers and people too poor to pay; they neither asked for nor received compensation from many of the victims.

Matthew Carey, who published the account of the charges, had hurriedly left the city. Fortunately, most of the citizens of Philadelphia knew the truth, and the mayor and the city council formally thanked Allen and his associates for the service they had rendered.

Richard Allen's fame spread as a minister and as a civic leader. He organized and dedicated Bethel African Methodist Church in Philadelphia in 1794. Later, African Methodist Episcopal churches were organized in Baltimore, Wilmington, and other cities of the United States.

The same trend toward independent organization manifested itself among Negro Baptists. Virginia Negroes established Baptist churches at St. Petersburg in 1776, Richmond in 1780, and Williamsburg in 1785. In Boston, Reverend Thomas Paul founded the first Baptist church of that city for Negroes in 1809.

There were other great Negro leaders in the religious field during the early days of our country, but Richard Allen is recognized as the spiritual pioneer of the Negro church and the first Negro bishop in America.

The Discipline of 1817 recorded that "on April 11,

1816, Richard Allen was solemnly set apart for the Episcopal office by prayer, and the imposition of the hands of five regularly ordained ministers, at which time the general convention held in Philadelphia did unanimously receive the said Bishop Allen as their Bishop, being fully satisfied of the validity of his Episcopal ordination."

CRISPUS ATTUCKS

?–March 5, 1770

Martyr for American Independence

Every school child knows the story of how the United States came to be. First there were the thirteen colonies, ruled by the English king and his ministers. But the colonists yearned for independence. They were not only heavily taxed, but were also forbidden to trade with any country except England. They were even forced to house and feed the British Redcoats who had been sent to keep them in order.

The Redcoats arrived in Boston in 1765, and remained year after year. The citizens grew angrier and angrier. Arguments and fights between the soldiers and the townspeople broke out as the situation became more tense.

Finally, on the night of March 5, 1770, the great bell

of the meeting house rang out, calling the people together. A fight between the Redcoats and a group of Boston citizens broke out over something which would have been an unimportant incident had tempers not been so short: one of the sentinels had knocked down a young boy. Hearing his cries, the people, armed with rocks and clubs, ran to face the Redcoats who stood with drawn bayonets.

A voice was heard above the crowd: "The way to get rid of these soldiers is to attack the main guard. Strike at their roots." It was the voice of Crispus Attucks. Attucks was a tall mulatto seaman who worked on the Boston docks where the heavily taxed British merchandise was unloaded. He had good reason to stand out against the British tyranny: he had once been a slave.

Encouraged by his words, the townspeople began their fight for freedom. The Redcoats, following the orders of their officers, fired into the crowd. The blood of Americans stained the snow.

Crispus Attucks was the first to fall; Samuel Gray, who had come to his aid, was next. Three more patriots rushed to help them: James Caldwell and Patrick Carr, both sailors, and Samuel Maverick, a youth in his teens. Caldwell died that day, Maverick the next morning, and Carr nine days later.

This tragedy, known as the Boston Massacre, so aroused the citizens that they demanded the removal of the British Lieutenant-Governor and the King's Council. Thus was won the first round in what was to become the American Revolution.

The men who died in that massacre are recognized today as the first martyrs to the cause of American Independence. The bodies of Attucks, Gray, Carr, Caldwell, and Maverick lay in state in Faneuil Hall. Hundreds of persons paid them tribute, and they were buried in a single grave. Later, a monument was erected on Boston Common to honor these heroes and patriots.

BENJAMIN BANNEKER

1731–1806

Astronomer

Benjamin Banneker was born near Baltimore, Maryland, November 9, 1731. His mother was a free woman and his father was a slave. His parents, being both thrifty and wise, worked together to buy the father's freedom. At a great sacrifice they were able to send their son to a private school near Baltimore that was open to both white and Negro children. Here Banneker studied hard and distinguished himself in mathematics.

The Bannekers' nearest neighbors were the Ellicotts, a Quaker family. Their son, George, became interested in Benjamin, loaned him books to read, and encouraged him to study mathematics and astronomy. So interested did young Benjamin become in the mathematical calculations relating to stars and constellations that he was able, by using tables of the ancients printed in Ellicott's books, to predict solar eclipses and other phenomena of the heavens. His own predictions and calculations were so accurate he was consulted by strangers as well as his own neighbors, and he found mistakes in the calculations of some of the leading authorities of his day!

After many years of watching the heavens and making weather predictions, he decided to prepare an almanac of his own. Without telling anyone his plans, he prepared his first almanac, which was published by Goddard and Angell of Baltimore in 1792, when Banneker was sixty-one years of age.

The almanac included the time of the eclipses, hours of sunrise and sunset, a tide table for the Chesapeake Bay and other nearby waters, festival days, holidays, and days for holding the Circuit Court. It also contained a list of medicines useful to help ward off diseases. Newspapers were not being printed or read widely at this time, so Banneker's almanac filled a real need.

Banneker was deeply interested in the plight of the Negro slaves and he printed much antislavery material, and extracts from the speeches of Thomas Paine, William Pitt, and C. J. Fox. Many of the other essays he printed dealt with the subject of war and its uselessness.

His ambition was to devise a plan that would put an end to all war and end slavery in the United States. He proposed the establishment of a Department of Peace with a Secretary of Peace in charge. He sent a copy of his almanac to Thomas Jefferson, who was then Secretary of State in George Washington's cabinet. Jefferson was so impressed by the almanac he sent a copy to Monsieur de Condorcet, secretary of the Academy of Sciences in Paris, who praised it warmly.

Meanwhile Banneker's friend George Ellicott had become a member of a commission to lay out the streets of Columbia (now Washington, D.C.), and recommended to Jefferson that Banneker serve on this commission. Jefferson submitted Banneker's name to George Washington, and Banneker was appointed. He worked closely with Major Pierre L'Enfant, an eminent French engineer, who was director of the commission. Washington, the seat of the United States government and home of the President of the United States, is today a city of great architectural beauty.

There was a great deal of confusion and dissatisfaction on this commission. Major L'Enfant received very little cooperation from the American engineers working with him and, in a storm of indignation, he finally left, taking with him the plans that had been so carefully worked out. But Banneker had seen the plans and was able to reproduce them in the fullest detail!

Earlier in his life, Banneker had built a clock patterned after a watch that had been given to him. This clock ran steadily and faithfully struck the hours, day and night, for more than twenty years. Travelers came to visit and check on the clock regularly because it was said to be the first *striking* clock built in the United States.

Benjamin Banneker's father lived to see some of his high hopes for his son come true; but his mother died earlier, and so did the girl whom he loved. Her tragic death saddened his life and caused him to find solace in books and study.

He kept a careful journal. This journal and copies of his almanacs can be found in the Maryland Historical Society and the Library of Congress. Copies of the Thomas Jefferson correspondence may be examined in the Rare Book Room of the New York Public Library. A tragic fire destroyed much of his precious writing before he died, on Sunday, October 9, 1806.

IDA WELLS BARNETT

1869–1931

Crusader Against Lynching

I DA B. WELLS was born in Holly Springs, Mississippi, in 1869. While she was still young, her parents died of yellow fever and Ida, the eldest of the children, had to bring up her brothers and sisters. She refused to allow them to be parceled out to neighbors and relatives; she kept the family together.

Meanwhile she managed to get an education. She attended Rust College in Holly Springs, and later Fisk University, where she became interested in journalism. In order to pay for her schooling, she taught in a nearby town during the week; on weekends she went home to Holly Springs to clean the house and wash and iron clothes for her brothers and sisters.

When she finished college, she taught in Memphis, Tennessee, but her interest in journalism persisted, for she had learned the power of the press. By stinting herself almost to the point of miserliness, she managed to buy half an interest in a little paper, the *Memphis Free Speech*. Soon she had built up the circulation so much that she was able to buy out her partner.

Once the paper was entirely hers, she put it to work for her ideals, and proceeded to write against the inequalities in education for Negroes in Memphis. The school authorities promptly dismissed her from the school system.

Now she was no longer a teacher, but a full-fledged journalist with a powerful weapon at her disposal. Her paper urged Negroes to leave Memphis and go north, where they would find better treatment and greater opportunities for employment. Her readers responded, and whole rows of houses were left vacant in the slum sections of the city.

She wrote blazingly against the frightful terror of lynchings, and began to keep what she called "The Red Record." In the years from 1890 to 1900, 1,217 Negroes were murdered or lynched and no single person stood trial. Ida Wells dedicated herself to the fight against mob violence and remained steadfast to the cause throughout her life.

She moved to New York and there worked on the *New York Age*, the Negro newspaper whose editor was T. Thomas Fortune, a good friend of Booker T. Washington. Her work brought her in contact with Frederick Douglass, Monroe Trotter, who was a leading Negro editor, and other prominent Negro men and women of the day.

In 1895 she married Ferdinand Barnett, a prominent lawyer of Chicago, and together they continued her crusade against lynching. She petitioned President Mc-Kinley in 1898 to take action against mob violence, and worked with political leaders to have legislation drawn up which would bring just punishment to lynchers.

Her activities in the field of social work laid the groundwork for the Urban League, an organization that helps Negroes from rural areas become adjusted to city life and promotes better interracial understanding in the United States. She was one of the petitioners for the conference in 1909 out of which grew the National Association for the Advancement of Colored People. And she founded the first federation of Negro Women's Clubs, which is why so many Negro women's clubs are named for her.

In 1931, Ida Wells Barnett died, after a life spent in battling the evils of lynching. To honor the constructive work she did for her people, a large housing development in Chicago has been named for her.

JAMES P. BECKWOURTH

1798–About 1867

Pioneer, Explorer, Mountain Man

DURING THE EARLY years of the nineteenth century, the trail blazers of the Rocky Mountain regions were known as the Mountain Men. Their exploits became legend. Never before or since in the history of our country—except among the very earliest settlers along the eastern coast—have men lived under conditions that demanded such physical courage, or such endurance of heat, cold, hunger, and thirst. Among the greatest of these Mountain Men was James P. Beckwourth, whose mother was a Negro slave.

In his autobiography, dictated to T. D. Bonner and published in 1856 by Harper and Brothers, Beckwourth tells of his birth in Virginia in 1798. He was one of thirteen children. His father, a white man, had been an officer in the Revolutionary War, and after the war was over the whole family, including the household of slaves, moved to an area near St. Louis, which came to be known as the Beckwourth Settlement.

While he was still young, his father apprenticed Beckwourth to a blacksmith. It was a hard life, and he quarreled violently with his master. When he was about eighteen years old he ran away, up the river to the mines of Galena. There the Indians, who supplied the miners with fresh meat, taught him to trap, hunt, and fish. From Galena he traveled to New Orleans, but was unhappy there, perhaps because of his mixed blood. He was accepted nowhere.

He returned to St. Louis, and joined an expedition, commanded by General Henry Ashley, which was part of the Rocky Mountain Fur Company. He was originally hired as a blacksmith, but soon became an expert trader. He got along well with the Indians, and began to trade not only in precious beaver pelts, but also in horses. He learned to be a good hunter, too, and provided fresh game to the men on the trail—wild turkeys, bear, deer, and buffalo. Sometimes he could find only stringy coyotes or small, fat prairie dogs. But they all shared their provisions, no matter what they were.

Beckwourth became a top-notch Indian fighter. He

was a crack shot who never wasted a bullet, and the wariest of scouts when the expedition traveled among hostile tribes. His greatest gift, however, was his ability to make friends among the less warlike Indians. He picked up their ways and quickly learned their tongues. Sometimes he spent the winter at a trading post near the Indian settlements, and bargained for the winter pelts of the beaver, when the fur was at its thickest and best.

One winter he and some others were separated from the main expedition. When they rejoined it, General Ashley was astonished not only to find Beckwourth alive, but to see the great bundles of valuable furs he had. Beckwourth and his companions had nearly died of exhaustion and starvation on the trail, but the young man's physical hardihood and great determination enabled him to lead them back to safety.

When they returned to St. Louis, Ashley offered Beckwourth a thousand dollars to carry a message to William Sublette, captain of his trappers, who was at the Fur Company trading post near the Great Salt Lake. Beckwourth made the trip and delivered the message. He wintered there with Sublette, and engaged in several skirmishes with the Blackfoot Indians over stolen horses. Sublette dispatched him to the Blackfoot country. He was to make friends and set up a fur-trading post among them, if possible.

Beckwourth was so successful that the Blackfeet accepted him as one of their own, and the Chief gave him his daughter for a wife. Later, he lived among the Crow Indians, and one family, believing him to be a son lost in childhood, adopted him. He was made a chieftain of the Crows, and bore the proud title of Bull's Robe.

But the great day of the Mountain Men and the fur companies was passing away. The men who knew the mountains turned mostly to scouting or to leading pioneers across the hazardous mountains and through the territory of the hostile Indians. Beckwourth was highly sought after as a scout, and was most successful at this pioneering work.

He was a scout for General Frémont during California's struggle for independence from Mexico. After the discovery of gold in California led to the Gold Rush, Beckwourth set up a store and trading post in northern California in the Feather River Valley, southeast of Mount Shasta.

Near the source of the Feather River and the Truckee River, Beckwourth discovered a pass, between two rugged mountain peaks, which bears his name to this day. It was an easier pass than others to the north and south. Thousands of gold seekers and pioneers passed over it, and the tracks of the Western Pacific Railway were laid through it. A plaque on a boulder in the pass commemorates Beckwourth's discovery.

After his years in California Beckwourth moved to Missouri. But like most of the old Mountain Men he could not be happy staying in one place. In 1859 he joined the stampede to Colorado, and in 1864, when he was sixty-two years old, he took part in the Cheyenne War. This was to be his last adventure, however; after the war he settled in Denver and there, sometime about 1867, the old pioneer died.

MARY McLEOD BETHUNE

1876–1955

Educator

MARY MC LEOD, the sharecropper's little girl, was playing by herself outside the big house. She heard the voice of Ben Wilson's granddaughter calling, "Mary, come into the house and see the beautiful doll Papa has brought me."

"I'm coming," Mary called back excitedly. "I'm coming right now. I've never seen a new doll! The only doll I ever had was the rag doll Mamma made for me."

Mary's eyes almost popped from her head when she saw the fabulous china-headed doll that Mr. Wilson had brought to his granddaughter from the city. Not only were there dolls in the little white child's bedroom, but a doll house, doll dishes, doll furniture, and every other kind of toy.

Mary had never seen such treasures as lay before her. Most fascinating of all was a big picture book lying open on a table. She put out a hand to pick it up, but the other child screamed, "Put that down; it's not for you," and snatched it up before Mary could actually touch it. "Besides," she said scornfully, as she clutched it, "a book wouldn't do you any good to look at, you can't read!"

Deeply hurt, Mary turned away, but in that moment was born an intense yearning to learn to read and write. Mary McLeod's father had brought his family to South Carolina to work for Ben Wilson, who owned not only the big house but all the rice and cotton fields for acres around. Mary was one of fourteen children, all of whom had to help their parents work the rice and cotton farm on shares with the Wilsons.

The McLeod family was deeply religious, and young Mary early thought of God as a friend who personally directed her life and watched over her. It seemed to her that He had especially prepared a feast of good things for her when one of the Wilson sisters, a member of the family in the big house, opened a school for Negroes in Maysville, South Carolina. It was under the direction of the Missionary Board of the Presbyterian Church.

Mary eagerly attended the school even though she

had to walk five miles from farm to town to get there, and her work in the fields prevented regular attendance. However, she was such a good student that, when she completed elementary school, a church benefactor in Denver, Colorado, made it possible for her to enroll in Scotia Seminary in Concord, North Carolina. Here she studied diligently and did domestic work to help pay her expenses.

Upon graduation, Mary received a scholarship to the Moody Bible Institute in Chicago. She had planned to become a missionary in Africa, but when she graduated, she found no openings for a Negro woman missionary in Africa. So she turned to teaching.

She was offered her first appointment as a teacher in Haines Normal and Industrial Institute, Augusta, Georgia. She felt she could be a missionary here just as well as in Africa, and she set to work with enthusiasm to teach, not only the pupils at the Institute, but also a large group of children she gathered from the streets of Augusta. She conducted a mission school on Sunday afternoons for these children. Here she was inspired by Lucy Craft Laney, the founder of Haines Institute, to start a school of her own for poor Negro girls.

Her next position was in Sumter, South Carolina, her own home state, and it was here that she met and married Albert Bethune, a fellow teacher. He encouraged her in her ambitions for a school of her own, but the way was not yet open for her. They moved to Savannah, Georgia, and spent a happy two years together there where their son, Albert McLeod Bethune, was born. From Savannah, they went to Florida, and her husband died there. Now more than ever she was determined to let nothing stand in the way of her plan to build a school of her own where she could teach and train poor Negro girls.

She went to Daytona Beach, Florida, where numerous wealthy families had vacation homes. She hoped she might interest them in her idea. She found an old empty shack, and with one dollar and fifty cents in cash, but millions of dollars worth of faith in her idea, she persuaded five little ragged girls to accept her as their teacher. She went to merchants, ministers, and other leaders, both white and Negro, and persuaded them to help her.

By faith and zeal, she succeeded in building a school which was dedicated on October 4, 1904. It was called the Daytona Educational and Industrial Training School. The first building was appropriately named Faith Hall, because it had been built through her great faith in God. In 1922, the Board of Education of the

Methodist Episcopal Church decided to merge their boys' school, Cookman Institute, founded in 1872 in Jacksonville, Florida, with Mrs. Bethune's girls' school. The two schools merged under the name Bethune–Cookman College, and although the school is affiliated with the Methodist Church, it remains nonsectarian.

This human dynamo not only ran a college, but dedicated her life to improving the lot of Negro women throughout the United States. She was called to Washington in 1934 to head the Office of Minority Affairs of the National Youth Administration (NYA), the first such post ever created for a Negro woman. Here she met President Franklin D. Roosevelt and, later, his wife, Eleanor Roosevelt, who became her close friend. They were both impressed with her deep sincerity of purpose and her dedication to the welfare of her people.

With the help of Mary Church Terrell, a famous Negro clubwoman, she organized the National Council of Negro Women, an organization of half a million women from every state in the United States. This organization, with permanent headquarters in Washington, D.C., works for the welfare of women all over the world.

She was selected by Ida M. Tarbell in 1931 as one of the fifty women who have "contributed most to the enrichment of American life." In 1935 she received the

Spingarn Medal, which is awarded yearly by the National Association for the Advancement of Colored People for "the highest achievement by an American Negro during the preceding year," in recognition for her devoted service to Negro youth. In 1949 she went to Winter Park, Florida, to receive an honorary degree of Doctor of Humanities from Rollins College. This was her ninth honorary degree. She received the Thomas Jefferson Award from the Southern Conference on Human Welfare for her work for Negro youth of the south, and in 1949, she journeyed to Haiti and was given the Order of Honor and Merit, Haiti's highest decoration. It was the first time in history the award was given to a woman.

She received the African Star from the Government of Liberia; she was given an audience with Pope Pius XII, as well as with the Lord Mayor of London. Perhaps the assignment which gave her the greatest personal satisfaction was her work at the San Francisco Conference for the Organization of the United Nations. She was sent as a consultant to help frame the Charter for the Declaration of Human Rights.

By the time of her death, on May 18, 1955, Bethune–Cookman College in Daytona Beach had become one of the foremost colleges in America. It is one of the few places in the south where interfaith and interracial meetings can be held in safety.

It is there that Mary McLeod Bethune is buried. Her name has been given to hundreds of Negro schools and Negro women's clubs not only in the United States but in Haiti, the Virgin Islands, and Africa.

GEORGE WASHINGTON CARVER

About 1860–1943

Scientist, Humanitarian

G EORGE WASHINGTON CARVER, born
in bondage about 1860 at Diamond Grove, Missouri,
never knew his mother or father. When he was only a
few months old, raiders stole him and his mother from
the plantation of Moses Carver. The mother was sold
and shipped away from her child forever, but Carver
managed to ransom the baby by trading a race horse
for him. The little boy was brought up on the Carver
plantation, and given the surname of Carver.

He showed signs of unusual intelligence, but there
was no Negro school close enough for him to attend.
Moses Carver sent him to Neosho, the Newton County
seat, in southwest Missouri. There George worked as

a farm hand to support himself, and studied in a one-room, one-teacher school. He received excellent grades and when he finished high school was determined to go to college.

After being rejected by many other colleges, young George Carver was accepted by Simpson College in Indianola, Iowa, as its first Negro student. Here, too, his record was outstanding. After graduation he was admitted to Iowa Agricultural College (now Iowa State University) at Ames, Iowa. He studied agricultural science there, graduating in 1894 and taking a master's degree in 1896. When his studies were completed, he was elected to the faculty of Iowa Agricultural College, the first Negro ever to serve on this faculty.

But his stay in Iowa was a brief one. Booker T. Washington heard of young Carver's remarkable record there, and invited him to the Tuskegee Institute in Alabama. Carver accepted, and became director of Tuskegee's department of agricultural research.

He knew that the salvation of the south's poverty-stricken population lay in the products of its farms. His great desire was to show the people of the south that they could diversify their crops, and not have to depend on a single money crop, such as cotton, tobacco, or rice. He was concerned with the people's physical welfare as well as their prosperity. He once said that the cure for the poor health of the southerners "grew in every road-side ditch. If the people would only learn to eat the green weeds that grew so abundantly there, their gaunt, undernourished struggle would be ended."

George Carver was a dedicated and patient researcher. He developed some three hundred products from the peanut, such as dyes, plastics, soap, ink, and many others now in common use. He also developed products from sweet potatoes, wood shavings, and cotton stalks. These were all products and by-products of the farms of the south. Carver was never interested in material gain, and rejected many offers from commercial outlets and businesses to patent his inventions or formulas, though he might have made a great fortune from them.

George Washington Carver won many honors during his long years of scientific research. He was made a fellow of the Royal Society of Arts in London in 1917, and awarded the coveted Spingarn Medal in 1923. In 1939, he was awarded the Theodore Roosevelt Medal for Distinguished Research in Agricultural Chemistry, with this citation: "To a scientist humbly seeking the guidance of God and a liberator to the men of the white race as well as the black." In 1940, the International Federation of Architects, Engineers, Chemists and

Technicians gave him a citation for distinguished service. In 1941 the University of Rochester conferred on him the degree of Doctor of Science, and the Catholic Conference of the South cited him for distinguished service to humanity.

During his later years he used his life savings of $33,000 to establish the George Washington Carver Foundation for Agricultural Research. He never married, and had no family ties when he died in 1943.

A memorial has been erected in his honor at Tuskegee Institute, along with a museum which holds thousands of mementos attesting to the love and esteem of people all over the world. The farm land near Diamond Grove, Missouri, where he was born and raised, is now maintained as a national monument by the United States government.

JOSEPH CINQUE

?–?

Mutineer for Freedom

I N THE SPRING of 1839, Joseph Cinque was among a group of young Africans who were seized and carried off to be sold into slavery. He was of royal blood, the son of a Mendi chief.

Surprised and caught off-guard, Joseph found himself packed in the filthy hold of a Portuguese vessel bound for Cuba. On arrival, fifty of the future slaves, including Cinque, were purchased by two Spaniards. They were to be sent from Havana to Principe on a chartered ship called the *Amistad*.

Young Cinque did not wish to be a slave for the rest of his life, so he took several trusted Africans into his confidence, and hatched a plot to gain their freedom.

One night, when the crew and officers of the ship

were asleep, Cinque and his companions seized all the weapons on board and killed the captain and the cook. They set the crew members adrift in a small boat, and ordered the ship's owners to steer the vessel back to Africa.

But the navigators tricked the Africans, and steered the ship away from Africa. They spent sixty-three days on the high seas, sailing due northwest. Many of the captives died from lack of food and water. Finally the *Amistad* arrived off Long Island, New York, and was convoyed by the United States Navy to New London, Connecticut, at pistol point.

Cinque and his companions were arrested and charged with the murder of the *Amistad*'s captain. The trial was headlined widely.

Abolitionists, hearing of the case, rushed to the defense of the Africans. They charged that since the Africans had been kidnaped they had the rights of free people everywhere to use whatever means they might find to obtain their freedom. Law students from nearby Yale University were excused from classes to attend the trial because of the many legal questions involved. The Africans made many friends among the faculty and students of Yale.

A committee was organized to collect funds for the

defense. This committee eventually developed into the American Missionary Society. President Martin Van Buren rejected an appeal to free the captives, but on March 9, 1841, after an eight-and-one-half-hour argument, the United States Supreme Court ordered Cinque and his fellow Africans to be freed. The young men acquired an education, aided by the abolitionists, before they returned to Africa in 1842.

FREDERICK DOUGLASS

1817–1895

Abolitionist, Orator

W<small>HY AM</small> I a slave? Why are some people slaves and others masters?" These were the questions that small Frederick Bailey asked himself over and over.

He was born in 1817 on a plantation on the eastern shore of Maryland; his mother was a "field hand," and his father a white man whom he never knew. When he was eight years old, his mother died.

As a child he suffered hunger and cruelty, but as he grew older he learned that not all black people were slaves, and that not all white people were cruel. One of his master's daughters was especially kind to him. She felt sorry for the motherless child, and arranged for him to be sent to Baltimore to serve in the household of her brother-in-law. There he became the special property of the small boy of the family. His young master's mother, Mrs. Auld, allowed the slave boy to listen while she read the Bible to her son.

One day Frederick summoned up his courage. "Mistress," he asked, "will you teach me to read?" His mistress was astonished that a slave should want to read. She knew the law against it, but he begged so earnestly that she finally agreed. "I will teach you, but we must be very careful that no one finds out. The master would be very angry if he knew," she said.

The lessons progressed rapidly until Mr. Auld discovered what his wife was doing. He ordered her to stop. "Teaching a slave to read leads to his learning to write. Then, the next thing, he'll run away," he told her. So Frederick's instruction ceased, but he pored over every bit of printing he saw, even the signs on the streets and in the store windows. He read with his young master while the little boy was studying. He was beaten when he was discovered copying from an old Bible and hymn-book late at night. But he persisted. When Frederick read books about liberty and freedom, he did not know what many of the words meant, but he read them just the same. With the same indomitable spirit, he taught himself to write.

Frederick Douglass

He was sent to live with another member of the family on whose estate a little Sunday school for the slaves was started. Frederick asked to teach it, but when his old master discovered that the boy was actually teaching the other slaves to read, the Sunday school was quickly broken up and Frederick was beaten again. His master began beating him regularly to try to break his spirit, but this was not possible. He was sent to work for Edward Covey, a farmer who was well known for his harsh treatment of defiant slaves.

Now his life was even more miserable, for besides hard work from sunup to sundown, he had to endure frequent floggings. He tried to run away but was caught, returned, and punished again. One day Frederick, a young man by this time, decided to defend himself against the cruel Covey. He flung him off, and when Covey saw that he was going to be beaten by Frederick he stopped, and never tried to whip him again. Frederick realized that in refusing to allow himself to be beaten he had become a man. This was the turning point in his life.

He continued his attempts to escape, sometimes alone, sometimes with others. He once wrote that he hated slavery so much that he "wished himself a bird, a beast, anything rather than a slave." Eventually, by careful planning and with endless patience, he got together some clothing, obtained some papers from a sailor who was tired of the sea, and set out for New York disguised as a sailor. Good fortune was with him, for the forged papers enabled him to escape detection. Frederick was free!

In New York he found free Negroes and others who helped him. He was introduced to David Ruggles, the secretary of the New York Vigilance Society, who advised him to leave New York and go to New Bedford, where he could find work as a caulker, a trade he had learned when he worked on the docks in Baltimore as a slave. Ruggles also suggested that he change his name. His mother had christened him Frederick Bailey, but it would be dangerous to use this name now. Frederick had planned to call himself Johnson, but he found there were many Negroes with that surname, so he asked his host in New York, who was also named Johnson, to make a suggestion. This man had just finished reading Sir Walter Scott's *Lady of the Lake*, and had been so impressed by the main character in the book that he immediately proposed that Frederick take the hero's name, Douglass. This is the name he bore for the rest of his life.

With his new name, Frederick Douglass began a new

life with the girl he loved. Among the friends in Baltimore who had given him invaluable aid in escaping was a young girl whose parents were free Negroes. Her name was Anna Murray, and she and Douglass had long hoped to be married. Loyal friends helped them and eventually they were married by the Reverend J. W. C. Pennington, a well-known Presbyterian minister in New York.

It was decided that the young couple should leave immediately for New Bedford. They rushed to catch the first stagecoach, but Douglass did not have enough money for their fare, so a kindly Quaker passenger came to their rescue, paid their fare, and directed them to a family of free Negroes in New Bedford.

Douglass immediately joined the Abolitionist Society and became active in it. He made his first speech against slavery in Nantucket in 1841 at the age of twenty-four. From then on he appeared at meetings on the same platform with Wendell Phillips, William Lloyd Garrison, Sojourner Truth, Harriet Beecher Stowe, Lucretia Mott, and countless other great men and women. He became a friend of John Brown, but took no part in Brown's ill-fated revolt.

During the early years of the War Between the States, the Union Army refused to accept Negroes into the ranks, but Douglass, who by that time had become an important figure in the abolition movement, went to Washington to see President Abraham Lincoln. He urged the President to recruit Negroes. "Why do you fight the rebels with only one hand when you might strike effectively with two?" he argued.

His own two sons, Charles and Lewis, were among the first Negroes to enlist. When the first units of Negroes were finally formed, Douglass addressed them with these stirring words: "Get an eagle on your button, a musket on your shoulder and a star-spangled banner over your heads." Thousands of Negroes, free and slave, flocked into Lincoln's army with this encouragement, and they made a great contribution to the war which was being fought, partly, in their behalf.

Douglass was sent to England to lecture against slavery, although he was legally still a slave, living daily in fear of being sent back to his master. While he was there his friends in America raised a "fund of one hundred and fifty pounds sterling" to purchase his freedom. His manumission papers, duly signed by his master, Mr. Auld, were presented to him at a large meeting in London.

After the war was over he devoted himself to working to attain the full rights of citizenship for Negroes, and for all people. He was one of the few men who supported women's suffrage, and he even stood on the lecture platform to defend women's right to the ballot. His wife, Anna, lived to hear him make one of the greatest speeches of his lifetime, at the dedication of a monument to Lincoln in Washington in 1876. She died shortly afterwards.

He was appointed by President Rutherford B. Hayes to serve as Marshal of the District of Columbia in 1877. He became a leader in the Republican party and was appointed by President James A. Garfield as Recorder of Deeds for the District of Columbia.

In 1884 he married again. His second wife, Helen Pitts, was a graduate of Mount Holyoke College. She was a great asset to him in his responsibilities as a public servant. In 1889 he was appointed to the post of United States Minister to Haiti. He died at his home, Cedar Hill in Anacostia, D.C., February 20, 1895.

In addition to a newspaper *The North Star*, Frederick Douglass published his autobiography, *My Bondage and Freedom*, which was later revised and called *Life and Times of Frederick Douglass*, as well as numerous newspaper articles and speeches.

CHARLES RICHARD DREW

1904–1950

Organizer of the Blood Bank

CHARLES RICHARD DREW was born in Washington, D.C., on June 3, 1904. He received his preliminary education at Dunbar High School, and went on to graduate from Amherst in 1926, with high honors. He attended McGill University Medical School in Montreal, Canada, where he won first prize in physiological anatomy, two fellowships in medicine, and honors in athletics.

In 1933, Drew received both his M.D. and Master of Surgery degrees from McGill, again with top honors. He served at the Royal Victoria Hospital and the Montreal General Hospital. In 1935 he returned to Washington to become an instructor in pathology at Howard University. He was soon promoted to Assistant in Surgery. In 1938 he was awarded a Rockefeller fellowship.

Drew did postgraduate work at the Columbia College of Physicians and Surgeons and received his Doctor of Medical Science degree in 1940. Drew's report of the Blood Plasma Project for Great Britain guided the later developments in this type of work, not only for the United States Army, but also for its allies.

In 1941, the American Red Cross set up blood donor stations to collect blood plasma for the armed forces, and Dr. Drew was appointed director of the project. After it had been successfully organized, he resigned to become the chairman of the surgery department at Howard University. He contributed numerous articles to medical journals on the subject of blood, and was recognized both nationally and internationally as an expert in his field.

Dr. Drew was killed in an automobile accident in April, 1950.

WILLIAM EDWARD
BURGHARDT DuBOIS

1868–1963

Leader, Scholar, Philosopher

WILLIAM E. B. DU BOIS was born in Great Barrington, Massachusetts, on February 23, 1868, of French Huguenot and Negro descent. His early schooling was in New England; and he continued his studies at Fisk University, where in 1888 he received an A.B. degree. In 1890 he obtained the same degree at Harvard University. He studied at the University of Berlin, then returned to take a Doctor of Philosophy degree at Harvard in 1895. His dissertation was "The Suppression of the African Slave Trade," which was published the next year as Volume I of the Harvard University Historical Series and used as a textbook in colleges all over the country.

William Edward Burghardt DuBois

Young DuBois taught first at Wilberforce University in Ohio, then at the University of Pennsylvania, where he published the classic study, *The Philadelphia Negro*. Later he went to Atlanta University, where for thirteen years he taught economics and history, and edited an annual on the problems of Negro Americans.

Although he was born shortly after freedom had been assured to all Negroes throughout the United States, he grew to manhood at a time of great oppression and increasing prejudice against his race. By 1905, while DuBois was still a comparatively young man, he decided something must be done to relieve the misery and degradation of his people. Under his leadership, twenty-nine young Negroes met in conference at Niagara Falls, New York, to launch an organization known as the Niagara Movement. Their aim was to protest against distinctions based on race and color, and to appeal to their fellow citizens to help build human society on the basis of human brotherhood.

Out of the Niagara Movement grew a much larger, stronger organization: the National Association for the Advancement of Colored People, founded on Lincoln's birthday, 1909. For twenty-four years Dr. DuBois edited *The Crisis*, the official magazine of the National Association for the Advancement of Colored People. He continued to teach and to write articles and books on the Negroes' past in Africa, their cultural inheritance, and their many living problems. In his long life he wrote nineteen books, among them many which have been used and respected by scholars everywhere. Some of the best known are *The Souls of Black Folk* (1903); a novel, *The Dark Princess* (1928); *Black Reconstruction* (1935); and *Black Folk: Then and Now* (1939).

During the Versailles Peace Conference following World War I, Dr. DuBois organized the First International Congress of Colored Peoples, later known as the Pan-African Congress, which met in Paris. Through his vision and leadership, African countries were encouraged to work toward full freedom and independence from European domination. He lived to see many of his plans realized in the emergence of independent African nations. More than thirty of them held seats in the United Nations General Assembly at the time of his death.

The honors Dr. DuBois won as a philosopher and writer included many honorary degrees from colleges and universities both here and abroad, and decorations from foreign governments. He was awarded the Spingarn Medal in 1920.

He was particularly revered by the African peoples

for encouraging them to study their ancient cultures and their contributions in past and present to all mankind, and to acknowledge before the world their great heritage. In 1962, at the invitation of the government of Ghana, Dr. DuBois went to live in Accra, where despite his great age he continued to work, this time as editor of the *Encyclopedia Africana*.

The next year, at the age of ninety-five, Dr. DuBois died in Accra. It was on August 27, 1963—the very day before the great Freedom March on Washington, led by the National Association for the Advancement of Colored People, which he helped to found so many years ago.

PAUL LAURENCE DUNBAR

1872–1906

Poet

As LONG AS he could remember, Paul Laurence Dunbar had wanted to be a writer. While in grammar school in Dayton, Ohio, he wrote poems and articles; in high school he became the editor of the school magazine, and was chosen to write the class song for graduation.

The Wright brothers were among his earliest supporters. They included many of Dunbar's poems in the little neighborhood paper they printed by hand in their basement. He was sixteen years old when his first published poem appeared in the *Dayton Herald*.

After he had read one of his poems at a session of the Western Writers Association in Dayton, one of the members encouraged Dunbar to publish his poems. He finally persuaded a small religious publishing firm to print a limited number of volumes which he agreed to sell himself. He peddled his first little book, *Oak and Ivy*, to his friends and to the passengers who rode the elevator he operated.

Dunbar made many loyal and devoted friends. When he went to Chicago to seek a job at the World's Columbian Exposition, he met Frederick Douglass, the great Negro abolitionist. Douglass helped Dunbar secure a small job, and the young poet wrote "The Columbian Ode" to commemorate the exposition.

Dr. H. A. Tobey of Toledo arranged for Dunbar to lecture to a large group of Toledo's leading white citizens. This lecture was so successful that it led to invitations from other large cities, where he sold many copies of his book.

A second volume of poems, *Majors and Minors*, was privately printed in 1895, and William Dean Howells enthusiastically reviewed it. Dunbar became famous overnight. The next year his *Lyrics of Lowly Life* was issued by Dodd, Mead and Company; it was his first book published by a commercial firm. Mr. Howells wrote the introduction. In 1897 Dunbar went to London for Queen Victoria's Diamond Jubilee, where he read his poems to large audiences. On his return he worked for a year as assistant in the Library of Congress in Washington, D.C.

Although Paul Laurence Dunbar is remembered largely for his dialect verses, he never intended to concentrate on dialect alone. He wrote prose as well as serious poetry, novels, short stories, essays, criticism, and short plays.

Among his published works are four novels: *The Uncalled* (1898), *The Love of Landry* (1900), *The Fanatics* (1901), and *The Sport of the Gods* (1902). His collections of short stories are *Folks from Dixie* (1898), *The Strength of Gideon* (1900), *In Old Plantation Days* (1903), and *Heart of Happy Hollow* (1904). He also wrote the lyrics used in eight musical shows, one of which, *Origin of the Cakewalk* (1898), was performed for an entire season in New York.

Forty of his poems were set to music by famous musicians of his time, including the Negro composers J. Rosamond Johnson and Samuel Coleridge-Taylor. Fifteen of his short stories appeared in such magazines as *Lippincott's, The Saturday Evening Post, The Independent,* and the Dayton, Ohio, *Tattler.* He wrote articles and essays for *Harper's Weekly, The Century Magazine, The Denver Post, Smart Set,* and other leading periodicals.

Paul Laurence Dunbar

Dunbar married Alice Ruth Moore of New Orleans in March, 1898. The following year he was awarded an honorary degree by Atlanta University. The poet died in 1906, and was buried in Dayton, Ohio, on Lincoln's birthday.

JEAN BAPTISTE POINTE
DuSABLE

About 1745–1818

Founder of Chicago

THE HONOR OF founding Chicago and of becoming its first permanent citizen, largely responsible for its early growth, belongs to Jean Baptiste Pointe DuSable, of French and Negro descent.

He was born about 1745—some thirty years before our Revolutionary War—in St. Marc on the island of Haiti. His mother, Suzanne, was a beautiful slave girl on a plantation on St. Croix. His father, mate on a pirate ship, the *Black Sea Gull*, stole her from her master and took her to Haiti, where she became free. He married her, and they had one son, who called himself by various names, with various spellings. This was a common practice then, but the most accepted form is as we have given it.

His mother was killed in a Spanish raid on St. Marc, and so his father took Jean to France, where he put him in a boarding school for boys near Paris. He became friends with another boy from a Caribbean island, Jacques Clemorgan of Martinique, who was his life-long companion.

When the two boys returned to Haiti, Pointe Du-Sable's father had given up his piracy and was dealing in coffee, rare island woods, and other island products. He bought a schooner, which he named the *Suzanne* for his dead wife, and the two young men sailed off in her to the New World, hoping to bring back new stores for the father's warehouse. On the way to America, in a hurricane, the *Suzanne* was wrecked, but the two young men escaped and were taken to New Orleans in another vessel.

Because of his color, DuSable was in constant danger in New Orleans either of being imprisoned as an es-caped slave or of being sold into slavery. He made friends with the Jesuit fathers, who hid him. Because he could not hire out to any of the trading companies as he wished, he built himself a small boat and escaped in it up the Mississippi River. His friend, Jacques, and a Choctaw Indian guide who spoke several native languages, paddled with him until they reached Saint Louis. Newly established (1763), it was a fort and a flourishing fur-trading center. DuSable stayed in the region for some time, learning to speak the language of the Illinois tribe, and to live and hunt like an Indian. He journeyed on—up the Illinois and across the Great Lakes into Canada. For a time he was in the pay of the British Governor in Detroit.

Back in Illinois, near Peoria, he lived among the Potawatami tribe, and there fell in love with an Indian maiden named Kittihawa—Fleet-of-Foot. In order to marry her he became a member of the tribe, purchased land, and settled among them as a farmer and trader. He not only became adept in Indian ways, but was an excellent businessman, in the manner of his French forebears. Only a man of wide interests and many activities would have left so many records and legal documents about himself throughout the Northwest territories.

During his trading ventures into the North, DuSable must have often crossed the short portage between the Des Plaines River and what is now known as the Chicago River, with its two branches flowing into Lake Michigan. He saw it would be an ideal trading point, and built a trading post on the north branch in 1772. Two years later he enlarged it into a five-room dwelling with a fireplace and brought his wife and son and her whole tribe of Potawatamis to settle in this area called Eschikagou, or sometimes Chikagou, by the Indians. There his daughter, Suzanne, named for her grandmother, was born—the first recorded birth in the settlement. Later the Indians used to say, "The first white man in Chicago was a Negro!"

DuSable added other buildings—barns, a forge and mill, bake- and smokehouses, and workshops. Around him other homes were built, gardens and fields planted. His trading post became known as the best one between St. Louis and Montreal.

During the troubles between the French and Indians and the British, and later, during our Revolutionary War, DuSable was suspected of being in alliance with the French and Indians of the area. He was arrested in 1778 and taken to Fort Mackinac at the head of Lake Michigan, but was later released, since there was no proof of his being influential against the British.

DuSable became an interpreter and guide of great note, sought by missionaries, trappers, hunters, and explorers who made Chicago their stopping-off place. So respected was he by the Potawatamis that they once proposed him as their chieftain. He was also the friend of the great Ottawa chief, Pontiac, and of Daniel Boone.

In 1800, at about the age of fifty-five, he sold his holdings to a trader from St. Joseph, Missouri, named Le Mai, who in turn sold them to John Kinzie, reputed founder of Chicago. The bill of sale to Le Mai, however, is recorded in the Wayne County Building in Detroit, proving DuSable's prior claim as founder of the second largest city in the United States. In 1804, during the Fort Dearborn Massacre, the Indian raiders spared the building that had been DuSable's home, out of respect, and perhaps believing that he still lived there. John Kinzie enlarged and improved the building, and lived in it, so the house truly became the first permanent dwelling in Chicago, as a bronze plaque at the corner of Dearborn Street and Wacker Drive tells.

DuSable moved with his son and namesake to St. Charles, a frontier town in Missouri, where he interpreted the Indian languages for pioneers passing through. In 1818, Jean Baptiste Pointe DuSable died and was buried among other pioneers of the West in St. Charles Borremeo Cemetery there.

DEBORAH GANNET

?–?

Soldier of the Revolution

DEBORAH GANNET of Massachusetts stands alongside Molly Pitcher and Betsy Ross as a heroine of the Revolutionary War. This woman was anxious to help America gain its independence from the British. When the call went out for "all able bodied men to come to the aid of their country," Deborah signed up even though she was a woman. She was so eager to serve that she disguised herself as a man, and joined a Massachusetts regiment under the name of Robert Shurtliff.

Deborah's disguise was so successful, and she conducted herself so courageously, that she won the respect and admiration of the entire regiment. She exhibited extraordinary heroism, and served throughout the war without revealing her sex.

When the war was over and won, Deborah applied to the Massachusetts legislature for military compensation as a consideration for her service. She was granted a retroactive pension of thirty-four pounds a year.

Deborah Gannet was cited for discharging the duty of "a faithful, gallant soldier, and at the same time preserving the virtue and chastity of her sex, unsuspected and unblemished, and was honorably discharged from the service."

Nothing is known of her life after her discharge from the Massachusetts regiment.

HENRY HIGHLAND GARNET

1815–1882

Educator, Orator

Henry highland garnet was born to slave parents on the plantation of William Spencer at New Market, Kent County, Maryland, on December 23, 1815.

When he was nine years old, he and his parents escaped to New Hope, Pennsylvania, where he had his first schooling. In 1825 the family moved to New York City, and took the name of Garnet. From 1825 to 1840, the boy continued his education, first under a tutor, Charles C. Andrews. Later he and another young Negro, Alexander Crummel, sought admission to the Academy at Canaan, New Hampshire. Mob action frustrated this plan, but Garnet was undiscouraged. He graduated from Oneida Institute, at Whitestown, New York, in

1840. He then settled in Troy, New York, where he not only taught school but served a church with a white congregation.

During the years before the Civil War, he was an active abolitionist. His radical speeches often alarmed even his fellow Negroes. His most famous statement was this call to Negroes to throw off the yoke of slavery: ". . . Awake, awake, millions of voices are calling you! Let your motto be resistance; no oppressed people have secured their liberty without resistance." During the Civil War, he went about relieving distress among the wounded and the imprisoned.

After the war, he served congregations in New York and Washington, and later became president of Avery College in Pittsburgh, where he was greatly admired and honored as an educator. In 1881 he was appointed Minister to Liberia, but he died there in February of 1882, only a few weeks after he arrived to take up the post.

ARCHIBALD HENRY GRIMKE

1849–1930

Lawyer, Author, Publicist

ARCHIBALD HENRY GRIMKÉ was born August 17, 1849, near Charleston, South Carolina. His father, Henry Grimké, a member of a prominent white family, was a famous southern lawyer. His mother, Nancy Weston, was a beautiful family slave. Nancy Weston was said to have been freed by her master before his death. At any rate, she sent her sons to a school for children of free Negroes conducted by a white man of Charleston.

After the Civil War, the boys attended a school for Negro children opened by Gilbert Pillsbury, Charleston's Reconstruction mayor, a northern abolitionist. The Pillsburys felt that the boys should go north for further education, and urged them to go to Lincoln University in Philadelphia, which at that time was conducted by whites.

Archibald was a brilliant student at Lincoln, and news of his success came to his father's sister Sarah. Sarah Grimké and her sister Angelina were unusual southern women—both had been leaders in the anti-slavery movement. Although Sarah Grimké had never seen any of her brother's children, she immediately invited her nephew to visit her.

In 1872, after he had graduated with honors from Lincoln, she helped him to enter Harvard Law School and paid his expenses for the first year of his two-year course. He won a scholarship which made it possible for him to finish. He was granted the LL.B. from Harvard in 1874, and soon became a partner in a law firm in Boston.

He was prominent in Negro affairs and particularly active in the Colored National League along with many famous New England Negroes. From 1883 to 1885 he was editor of *The Hub*, a newspaper devoted to the welfare of the Negro. In 1891–92 he wrote for the *Boston Herald*, the *Boston Traveler*, and also the *Atlantic Monthly*. He served as American consul to Santo Domingo from 1894 to 1898, and as president of the American Negro Academy from 1903 to 1916. Here he published many pamphlets and articles urging full equality for Negroes. He worked for equality for women, and also for Indians, Chinese, and other minorities.

He wrote biographies of William Lloyd Garrison (1891), Charles Sumner (1892), and Télémaque (Denmark) Vesey, the leader of the Charleston slave uprising of 1822 (1901); and many works protesting racial discrimination. Among these are *The Ballotless Victim of One-Party Government* (1913), *The Ultimate Criminal* (1915), and *The Shame of America, or, The Negro's Case Against the Republic* (1924).

He was an officer of the National Association for the Advancement of Colored People, and was awarded its Spingarn Medal in 1919. He was also a trustee of the Emmeline Cushing Estate, a foundation for Negro education, president of the Frederick Douglass Memorial and Historical Association, and a member of the Authors' Club of London and the American Social Science Association.

He died in Washington, D.C., where he had lived since 1905, on February 25, 1930.

WILLIAM C. HANDY

1873–1957

Musician, Composer of the Blues

W̲ILLIAM C. HANDY was the son of
Elizabeth Brewer and Charles Bernard Handy. He was
born in Florence, Alabama, and attended a school where
one of the teachers was a musician. He introduced
young Handy to the choruses of Wagner, Bizet, and
other great musicians. The music that most appealed to
the boy was the harmonizing in the barbershops and
on street corners and at picnics, and the great harmonies
of the spirituals sung in the African Methodist Church.

His father was a minister of that church and the
parents had intended William for a preaching career,
but while still a very young boy he showed his great
musical talent. In spite of his father's disapproval, he
purchased a cornet for $1.75 from a friend and secretly

arranged for lessons. Only his mother never laughed at his first awkward attempts on the cornet or at his ambition to play it as well as Claude Seals, a famous Negro cornetist of the day. The boy, William, had heard him play solos and accompaniments during his appearance with their church choir in Florence, which inspired him to take up the instrument seriously.

Because of his father's belief that professional musicians led a sinful life, and because the family was too poor to give him further education, young William left home on foot with his trusty cornet under his arm. He trudged the long way from Florence to Birmingham, where he taught school for two years. Then for a while he worked in the Bessemer Iron Works because he earned better wages there. Many of the harmonies he heard sung by the mill laborers he used in his "blues" in later years.

During the panic of 1893, when the whole country was in the depths of a depression and general unemployment put him and thousands of other iron workers out of work, Handy organized a quartet of musicians to go to the Columbian Exposition—a world's fair—in Chicago. Through the kindness of a switchman and a railroad guard, Handy and his three companions rode as far as St. Louis, Missouri, in a box car. Times were hard there, too, and the quartet was desperately poor. That night in a tavern, Handy heard a young man singing:

"Sometimes my heart grows weary of its sadness,
  Sometimes my heart grows weary of its pain . . ."

He grabbed a guitar from a man sitting near him and joined in the song. He poured into it all the weariness and hunger and heartbreak he had known since leaving Birmingham. The crowd applauded and clamored for more. This, according to Handy himself, was the occasion that gave "birth to the blues."

Although his quartet venture at the World's Fair was not an unqualified success, from that time on the young musician prospered. Returning south, he became a music teacher, then, in Alabama, was made a band leader and solo cornetist with Mohara's Colored Minstrels. Soon he had organized his own large band.

During a dance for white people in Mississippi, Handy observed that they were most enthusiastic about dancing to a small combination of his musicians—a mandolin, a guitar, and a bass viol. This was a group familiar throughout the south for Negro singing and dancing, and so he began to use it more and more when presenting his own compositions.

William C. Handy

Handy moved from Mississippi to Memphis, Tennessee, and there he began collecting tunes and experimenting with them. Soon he was putting this music on paper, and it was on Beale Street in Memphis that most of his compositions were written.

During the mayoralty campaign in 1909, three men ran for the mayor's office, and each candidate had his own band. Handy campaigned with his band for Edward Crump, who not only won as mayor, but went on to later become a United States congressman. As a campaign song, Handy had written *Mr. Crump Blues*, and at the close of the triumphant campaign, Handy found his band established as the most popular in Memphis. He transformed the campaign song into *The Memphis Blues*.

When he failed to find a publisher for it, he issued a thousand copies himself. Unfortunately, he sold another man the rights to orchestrate it for one hundred dollars, and so he could not include this song in the 1926 collection of his compositions, published by his own publishing company.

Among the sixty or more most popular compositions by William C. Handy are those most frequently played and familiar to all lovers of jazz: *The Memphis Blues, The St. Louis Blues, Beale Street Blues, The Mississippi*

78

Blues, and *The Joe Turner Blues*. In addition to secular songs, Handy harmonized and published excellent versions of the Negro spirituals. His *Evolution of the Blues* was performed in 1924 by Vincent Lopez at a jazz concert at the Metropolitan Opera House in New York City. And, in 1928, William C. Handy presented a concert at Carnegie Hall illustrating the development of Negro music, from the drums of Africa through the spirituals to present-day jazz.

A park in Memphis, part of the old Beale Street he made famous, is named in his honor. He was married in 1898 to Virginia Price, and six children were born to them.

William C. Handy died in 1957, but his songs—especially the most popular one of all, *The St. Louis Blues*—are still sung and played by orchestras and bands around the world.

FRANCES ELLEN WATKINS
HARPER

1825–1911

Abolitionist, Poet

Frances ellen watkins was born of
free parents in Baltimore, Maryland, in 1825. Orphaned
at the age of three, she was cared for by an aunt. She
attended a school kept by her uncle, where her literary
talent was first revealed. After Frances finished her
schooling, she became a teacher in schools in Ohio and
Pennsylvania.

Moved by the Negroes' bid for freedom, she became
active in the work of the Underground Railroad. Her
commanding appearance and talent for expressing herself eloquently and forcefully was quickly recognized
by the leaders of the abolitionist movement, and she became one of their best and most popular lecturers, and

one of the most devoted workers for the abolition of slavery.

In 1854, the Anti-Slavery Society of Maine engaged her as a permanent lecturer. After the publication of the Emancipation Proclamation, Frances Ellen Harper traveled, spoke, and read her poetry in all parts of the country.

She published several booklets of her poems, which sold into the tens of thousands of copies. The most widely quoted of her poems is "Bury Me in a Free Land," which reads:

Make me a grave where 'er you will,
  In a lowly plain or lofty hill;
Make it among earth's humblest graves,
  But not in a land where men are slaves.

I ask no monument, proud and high,
  To arrest the gaze of the passers-by;
All that my yearning spirit craves,
  Is bury me not in a land of slaves.

She was the first Negro woman to publish a novel—*Iola Leroy: The Shadows Lifted*, in 1860. Her other published works include *Moses: A Story of the Nile*, 1869; *The Dying Bondsman; Eliza Crossing the Ice;*

Frances Ellen Watkins Harper

Poems on Various Subjects, 1854; *Poems*, 1871; and *Sketches of Southern Life*, 1872.

She toured the country, north and south, and also Canada, where she was very well received. She spoke to many of the newly freed slave women of the south, encouraging them to learn to read and write and try to make comfortable homes for their families.

She married Fenton Harper of Cincinnati, and restricted herself mainly to her home while he was living. After his death, she resumed her activities among the women of America, particularly the Women's Christian Temperance Union. She traveled throughout the north, lecturing for this organization.

Eleven years after her death, at the World's Women's Christian Temperance Union meeting held in Philadelphia in November, 1922, she was accorded a signal honor. Her name was placed on the Red Letter Calendar beside the names of Frances E. Willard, Lady Henry Somerset, and other staunch supporters of temperance.

MATTHEW ALEXANDER
HENSON

1866–1955

Co-Discoverer of the North Pole

THE FIRST MAN to stand at the top of the world was Matthew Alexander Henson. As a trail-breaker for Rear Admiral Robert E. Peary, Henson reached the North Pole forty-five minutes before the leader of the expedition, on April 6, 1909. But he had spent years preparing for that moment.

Henson was born in Charles County, Maryland, in 1866. He was orphaned quite young, and at the age of eleven he ran away from a cruel stepmother. He went to Washington, where he worked as a dishwasher. His immense longing to become a sailor led him to tramp to Baltimore. He wandered among the huge docks and warehouses, and gazed at the ocean-going vessels. He signed as cabin boy on the *Katie Hines,* bound for Hong Kong.

The captain showed an interest in young Matthew, and taught him not only a great deal about navigation and piloting a ship, but also reading and writing. He spent five years sailing on the *Katie,* only leaving when the captain died.

Matt came ashore, and while working as a handy man in a clothing shop met Robert E. Peary, an engineer for the Navy. Peary liked the boy, and asked Matt to accompany him to Nicaragua as his personal attendant. Matt accepted, and was soon promoted to the surveying crew as field helper. He and Peary worked and traveled together for the next twenty-three years.

On their return from Central America, Peary told Henson that he planned to go to Greenland to explore the northern ice cap, but that he had no money to pay his companion because he had failed to find financial backing for the expedition. Matt offered to go without pay.

In 1888 Peary, Henson, and a number of other explorers set out for Baffin Bay. Henson soon proved himself the most useful member of the party; he handled a hammer and saw easily, drove the dog teams well, and picked up the Eskimo language quickly. Much of what he learned on this first trip was invaluable in their later Arctic explorations. When they returned to New York, Peary was determined to raise funds for an expedition to the North Pole.

Peary and Henson together made seven unsuccessful attempts to reach the Pole, and Peary made one alone. Between trips, Peary lectured throughout the country on the Arctic, while Henson worked in the Arctic section of the Museum of Natural History in New York. They had brought two huge meteorites and many other scientifically important contributions to the museum. During these years many people became interested in an American expedition to the North Pole, sufficient funds were raised, and Peary was provided with a ship, the *Windward*. Their failures only made the two men even more determined to reach their goal.

On July 8, 1908, Peary and Henson sailed again, this time in a new ship, the *Roosevelt*. They established a base on Cape Columbia, four hundred uncharted miles from the top of the world. Six months later, they were only one hundred and thirty miles from their objective. The supporting party was sent back to the base and Henson pushed ahead as trailblazer. Peary and four Eskimos brought up the rear. By April 5 they were only thirty-five miles from their goal. Now they were more aware than ever that a sudden Arctic storm, a miscalculation of direction, or separation in the vast wastes, might end in death for them all.

On April 6, 1909, however, Peary wrote in his logbook: "Arrived here today, 27 marches from Cape Columbia, I have with me 5 men, Matthew Henson, colored, Ootah, Egingwah, Seegloo, and Ooqueah, Eskimos; 5 sledges and 28 dogs. The expedition under my command has succeeded in reaching the POLE . . . for the honor and prestige of the United States of America."

As he surveyed the frozen wilderness, Peary turned to Matt Henson, and said: "This scene my eyes will never see again. Plant the Stars and Stripes over there, Matt —at the North Pole."

And so Matthew Henson, who had been indispensable in this great discovery, planted the American flag where there is no east, no west, no north—only south.

Peary was honored by being made a rear admiral. Henson was decorated by Congress and received a gold medal from the Chicago Geographical Society; a building on the campus at Dillard University in New Orleans was named for him. On the forty-fifth anniversary of the discovery of the North Pole, the Negro explorer was honored by President Eisenhower at the White House.

Young Americans, too, can take pride in Henson's and Peary's tremendous courage, for exploration into the Arctic wastes was as hazardous then as flight into outer space is now. Henson belongs to that small company of searchers into the mysteries of our world and of our universe for whom our admiration must be unbounded.

JAMES WELDON JOHNSON

1871–1938

Lawyer, Poet, Educator

J AMES WELDON JOHNSON was born in Jacksonville, Florida, in 1871. His mother was an intelligent, ambitious West Indian woman with a great love for music. She encouraged her two sons in their ambitions, and both of them became famous, James Weldon as a writer and a fighter for the rights of his people; his brother J. Rosamond as a composer of popular music, harmonizer, and recorder of the music of the great Negro spirituals.

James Weldon Johnson received his early education in Jacksonville, then went to Atlanta University where he received his Bachelor of Arts and Master of Arts degrees. He returned to Jacksonville as principal of an elementary school, and became determined to give young Negroes of that city a chance at higher education. When he had a class of particularly bright eighth-graders, he introduced high-school courses and provided efficient teachers. His school was eventually accepted as the first accredited high school for Negro children in the city.

Johnson studied law and was admitted to the Florida bar in 1897. He practiced law in Florida until he moved to New York in 1901. There he collaborated with his brother in writing the lyrics for many light operas and popular songs, for which his brother became famous. The brothers also gathered the material for their remarkable collection of spirituals, and James Weldon wrote an illuminating account of the history of Negro music as a foreword to it. These young men did a lot to preserve and make popular this great musical contribution to our culture in *The Book of American Negro Spirituals* and the *Second Book of American Negro Spirituals*.

In 1920 Johnson, while working as the Executive Director for the National Association for the Advancement of Colored People, went to Haiti to investigate misrule by United States administrators and the pitiful plight of the people there. His findings were published in the *Nation*; a Naval Board of Inquiry was set up; a congressional investigation was promised; and better administrative methods and concern for the welfare of the people were established.

Johnson also worked as a journalist, contributing editorials to the *New York Age*, and writing articles and poetry which appeared in many periodicals. His best poetry is collected in *Fifty Years and Other Poems* and *God's Trombones*. He also edited several anthologies of Negro writing, wrote a novel, *The Autobiography of an Ex-Colored Man*, and his own inspiring autobiography, *Along This Way*, in 1933.

He was killed in an automobile accident near his summer home in Maine in 1938. His greatest memorial is, perhaps, the splendid and popular hymn *Lift Every Voice and Sing*, for which his brother wrote the music. He won the Spingarn Medal in 1925.

EDMONIA LEWIS

1845–1890

Sculptor

E DMONIA LEWIS was born near Albany, New York, of mixed Negro and Indian parentage. The future artist was adopted from an orphanage and educated by abolitionists at Oberlin, Ohio, from 1859 to 1863. As far as is known, Edmonia Lewis was the pioneer Negro sculptor. She showed artistic talent at an early age, and was trained in the studio of Edmund Brackett of Boston.

Her first exhibited works were a medallion head of John Brown and a bust of Robert Gould Shaw, who led the first all-Negro regiment in the Civil War. These were shown at the Soldiers' Aid Fair in Boston in 1865.

Edmonia Lewis was fortunate in that her patrons recognized her talent, and she was sent to study with the Story family in Rome, where she became proficient in the fashionable neoclassic style of the day. Here she produced many figures, portraits, and symbolic groups directly in marble. On her return to the United States she executed a number of commissions. Among these were busts of Wendell Phillips, Harriet Hosmer, Charlotte Cushman, and one of Henry Wadsworth Longfellow, which was done for the Harvard College Library.

She was both talented and imaginative as a sculptor, and a number of her works represent Biblical or literary subjects. Best known among these are *Hagar* (1866), *Hiawatha* (1865), *The Marriage of Hiawatha* (1865), *The Departure of Hiawatha* (1867), *Madonna and Child* and *Forever Free* (1867). Miss Lewis exhibited in Rome in 1871 and at the Philadelphia Centennial in 1876.

Edmonia Lewis spent most of her life after 1876 in Rome, and died there in 1890.

JAN ERNEST MATZELIGER

1852–1889

Inventor of Shoe-Lasting Machine

A s ELIAS HOWE was to the sewing machine, so was Jan Matzeliger to the shoe-lasting machine. They both did the impossible." This quotation is taken from an article in *The Three Partners*, December, 1918, a magazine published by The United Shoe Machinery Corporation in Boston, Massachusetts.

Jan Matzeliger was born in Paramberio, Dutch Guiana, September 15, 1852. His father put him to work at the age of ten in the government machine works where he served as an apprentice. As soon as he became of age, he married a native girl and emigrated to the United States. They settled in Lynn, Massachusetts, in 1878.

Because of his experience in the machine shops of

Dutch Guiana, he found work at once in the factory of Harney Brothers, a shoe manufacturing concern. While working in the factory he overheard a workman say that "no man can ever build a machine that will last shoes unless the machine had fingers like a laster, which is impossible." This was a challenge to young Matzeliger, and he immediately started thinking about such a machine.

He questioned the men about the statement, as he watched the motions of their hands while they gripped the leather and sewed it at the same time. The more he watched the motions, the more he felt there must be a way. The men jeered at him, which made him more determined than ever to prove his belief.

He rented a cheap room over the old West Lynn Mission, and began experimenting at night after work. He used pieces of wood, old cigar boxes, and other scrap materials, and for six months he worked to build his model machine. Each day he watched the hands of the men as they stitched the leather, pleating it around the toe and heel of the shoes as they sewed, and each night he went back to his crude machine. He worked early and late, practicing and experimenting with first one idea and then another, with one object always in mind—to make a machine which could imitate as closely as possible the action of the fingers on the hands of the shoe-lasters at the factory.

At the end of six months he had a very crude model which worked. This made him certain that he was on the right track. He was offered $50 for the model, but he refused. For four years he worked and finally succeeded in making a model which, when completed in September, 1880, was capable of pleating the leather around the toe and heel of a shoe. When this became known, he was offered $1,500 for the machine, which he again refused.

He was not discouraged, though he was extremely poor and his health began to fail. He began work on a third machine, which was completed and patented March 20, 1883.

Shortly afterward, a hand-method lasting-machine company was formed by several men who became interested and helped Matzeliger financially. Matzeliger was still not satisfied with his machine and continued to work to perfect it. Finally he completed a fourth machine, which held the last in position and moved it forward, while other parts punched the leather and drew it over the last, fitted the leather at toe and heel, fed nails into position so the operator could drive them, and did all this so smoothly that a shoe could be completed in the space of one minute.

The strain of overwork and the frustration of poverty were too much, however. Matzeliger's health began to fail not long after the lasting machine was finished. He developed tuberculosis, and after a lingering illness he died on August 24, 1889, at the age of thirty-seven.

He bequeathed his stock to the North Congregational Church in Lynn, of which he was a member. His patent, and the stock in the company formed by the men who had helped him, became by 1904 valuable enough to pay off the mortgage on the church.

HUGH NATHANIEL MULZAC

1886–1971

Skipper

O<small>N</small> OCTOBER 27, 1942, during World War II, a Liberty ship, the *Booker T. Washington*, was launched in California. The ship's captain was Hugh Nathaniel Mulzac, who had already circled the globe fifteen times by sea. The crew was unique in that one half of the men where white and the other half colored. This was the first ship in the Merchant Marine service to have an integrated crew and a colored captain. Later three other such ships had colored masters.

Hugh N. Mulzac was born in the British West Indies. After attending school there, he went to the Swansea Nautical College in South Wales, and studied ocean navigation, since he had always been interested in a career on the sea. He was in his teens when he signed for his first voyage, on a Norwegian barque. When he was twenty-five he came to the United States and became a citizen. He attended the Shipping Board School in New York, where he studied navigation and wireless techniques and earned his second mate's license for both steam and sailing vessels. He also took a course from the I. C. S., and holds a diploma for ocean navigation and wireless from that school. In World War I, he carried war matériel to the Allies and after the war, in 1920, he received his master's papers from the steamboat inspectors. But there were few opportunities for a colored man to sail as a captain, so he had to take whatever position his color permitted. In 1922 he became captain of the S. S. *Yarmouth* of Marcus Garvey's Black Star line.

At the beginning of World War II Mulzac helped ship matériel to the British in Egypt, since he could not get an assignment from the United States Shipping Administration. It was only after pressure from a Negro organization, and the passage of President Roosevelt's Fair Employment Practices Act, that Mulzac became the captain of the *Booker T. Washington.*

His ship and crew proved that colored and white people could work together successfully. They braved enemy submarines to carry men and matériel through the waters of the North Atlantic to Europe.

The *Booker T. Washington* made twenty-two round-trip voyages between the United States and various ports and battle areas from 1942 to 1947. The officers and crew had faith in Captain Mulzac's ability. Not just the colored people, but all Americans were proud of the leadership of Captain Hugh Nathaniel Mulzac, Master Mariner of World War II.

POMPEY

?–?

Slave Hero of Stony Point

URING THE AMERICAN Revolution, Stony Point was a strategic fort on the Hudson River. The Americans had occupied it in 1776 and put up a blockhouse, but in May of 1779 the British captured it from them and fortified it even more strongly. In July of that year General Washington determined to retake Stony Point. He ordered General Anthony Wayne and a picked force of light infantry to recapture the fort.

Stony Point was a rocky promontory on the west side of the Hudson. At high tide it was cut off from the mainland, and at low tide it could be reached only by a well-guarded road across the marshes. Wayne and his men faced a difficult task.

Fortunately there was someone who could help them. A patriotic farmer in the neighborhood had a slave, Pompey, who often went back and forth between the British and American lines. The British soldiers at Stony Point received him kindly, and even bought strawberries and cherries from him. Pompey became a favorite with the garrison, for the British soldiers had no idea that he was reporting regularly to his master who, in turn, passed the important information on to Generals Wayne and Washington.

One day a Redcoat asked Pompey, "Why do you come only at night?"

"It's corn-hoeing season," answered Pompey. "I cannot come with the fruit in the daytime." The British gave Pompey the countersign so that he could pass the sentries in the evening.

On the day of the battle planned by General Wayne, Pompey had something no one else could have obtained without arousing suspicion—the countersign for entry to the Stony Point garrison.

Wayne ordered his forces to advance in the evening of July 15, 1779, at 11:30 P.M. Pompey cleared the way for the assaulting forces. He and two other strong men, disguised as farmers, moved ahead of the column. Challenged by the first sentry, Pompey gave the countersign. His companions seized and bound the guard, and Wayne's forces moved in, undiscovered, until they were within shooting distance of the pickets on the Point. The skirmish ended quickly, and Wayne sent this word to General Washington: "The fort and Colonel Johnson's garrison are ours. Our officers and men behaved like men who are determined to be free."

Washington and Wayne praised the soldiers, and Congress awarded gold and silver medals to individual officers and men. But Pompey, even though his shrewd actions had assured the success of the most complete surprise in our military history, was soon forgotten. Only his master rewarded his service to America—by giving him a horse to ride and never exacting any more labor from him.

GABRIEL PROSSER

1775–1800

Freedom Seeker

SLAVERY WAS HARD and it was cruel. Many slaves lived for only one purpose—to achieve freedom—and they were willing to risk their lives to escape. Many others, among them great leaders of the Negro people, plotted revolts. Over three hundred such revolts occurred before the Civil War. One of the most brilliantly organized was the "Great Gabriel Conspiracy" at Richmond, Virginia, which was led by a twenty-four-year-old slave, Gabriel Prosser.

Gabriel Prosser was born into slavery the year that the Revolutionary War began. Revolt against tyranny was in the air. Gabriel must have breathed a longing for freedom in his first breath.

Although he could neither read nor write, he was a

deep thinker and a natural leader. He listened to the talk among the planters, and dreamed of freedom. He found out from their conversations that Negroes outnumbered whites in and around Richmond. He also knew that there were many Quakers, and free Negroes, and some Frenchmen, who would not oppose the slaves in their fight for freedom.

When he was twenty-four years old, he began to make active plans for freedom. He spent the summer meeting secretly with his fellow slaves, sometimes in a tannery, a cabin, a smokehouse, or a barn; always a different location for each meeting. They decided that harvest time would be the best time to move. Food would be plentiful in the fields and woods, so those obliged to hide would not starve.

Prosser felt that if a group of slaves could take the arsenal in Richmond, others in surrounding counties would join them, and the Quakers and freedmen would not oppose them. Gabriel and his brother Martin planned a three-way invasion of Richmond. There would be a thousand men with them, but their only weapons would be blades of scythes cut in half, bayonets made of kitchen knives, slingshots, clubs, stones, and other clumsy instruments. The women would be similarly armed. They relied on surprising the enemy in taking over the arsenal, which was well stocked with guns and powder. Armed with guns, they could soon subdue the whites. Then Negroes from the country around Richmond would surely join them.

Their plans were well laid. The time was set for September 1, 1800, between midnight and dawn. All was ready except the weather. The night of the rendezvous a storm such as Richmond had never seen broke over the city. The thunder and lightning struck terror in the conspirators' hearts, and torrents of rain blocked their way as creek beds boiled over and swamps were flooded. Though Prosser had expected thousands, only a handful of slaves gathered at the meeting place. His ranks depleted by the raging storm, he dismissed them with the word that he would call them together for another attempt.

But before he could set another date, two slaves betrayed Prosser's plans. The authorities were so astounded at the scope of the conspiracy that they set up cannon around the capitol building, and called out a cavalry troop to guard the city. Then they began systematically to round up as many of the plotters as they could find. Some were hanged on the spot. Many slaves, innocent and guilty alike, were rushed to trial and executed. Hoping to set an example, the city authorities meted out jail sentences and whippings, and put some in chains.

Finally Prosser himself was captured. With his head held high in defiance, he was brought to Richmond. He and his companions had made a pact to die silent, but one of the men who was tried with Gabriel said, "I have nothing more to offer than General Washington would have had to offer had he been taken by the British officers and put to trial by them. I have ventured my life in endeavoring to obtain the liberty of my countrymen, and I am willing to be a sacrifice to their cause, but I beg, as a favor, that I may be immediately led to execution. I know that you have predetermined to shed my blood. Why then all this mockery of a trial?"

The United States *Gazette* spoke of Gabriel Prosser's composure and heroism. This courageous seeker of freedom was hanged on October 7, 1800. He was firm and confident, and not once did he whine or betray the names of any of his comrades in the plot. The seeds that he sowed for freedom took root, and sixty-five years after his death his people were freed.

NORBERT RILLIEUX

1806–1894

Inventor, Scientist

Norbert rillieux's birth record, on file in the city of New Orleans, reads: "Norbert Rillieux, quadroon libre, natural son of Vincent Rillieux and Constance Vivant, born March 17, 1806. Baptized in St. Louis Cathedral by Père Antoine."

His father was a well-to-do engineer and, as was customary at this time, he sent his son to Paris to study. Norbert was a brilliant student and at once showed an extraordinary aptitude for engineering. He became an instructor of applied mechanics at L'Ecole Centrale in Paris at the age of twenty-four.

In the same year, 1830, he published a series of papers on steam-engine work and steam economy. These created favorable attention in scientific circles all over Europe.

He had always been interested in the sugar-refining process. He remembered the gangs of sweating Negro slaves painfully pouring and ladling boiling sugar-cane juice from one steaming, open kettle to another, and it was his dream to perfect a modern method of sugar refining.

After much study, Rillieux solved the problem by linking the vacuum pans together in a series so that the vapor heat in the first pan could be applied to succeeding pans to evaporate their contents as well. The principles involved in this plan laid the foundation for all modern industrial evaporation.

But he was unable to interest French machinery manufacturers in his invention. It took twenty years for the French sugar-beet industry to adopt his plan, but the idea caught on in America. He was offered the post of Chief Engineer in Edmund Forstall's New Orleans sugar factory. Rillieux accepted the offer and returned to America, but because of a disagreement he quit the job after a short time.

In 1834 he installed the first working model of his triple-effect evaporator on the plantation of Zenon Ramon, in Louisiana. The machine failed, but Rillieux was not discouraged. In 1843, a second plantation owner, Theodore Packwood, encouraged Rillieux to design another triple-effect evaporator. This one was built by Merrick and Towne of Philadelphia. The machine was installed on Packwood's Myrtle Grove plantation in 1845 and was a complete success. Authorities agree that this installation was the first successful factory scale multiple-effect evaporator.

In the United States, Rillieux's apparatus was immediately recognized as revolutionizing the manufacture and refining of sugar.

Soon other Louisiana factories installed the system, and it was proved that the new evaporating system was responsible for producing a superior sugar product at greatly reduced cost. The sugar-refining firms that won first and second prizes for the best sugar of 1846 were both using Rillieux equipment.

From 1845 to 1855 Norbert Rillieux's name was well-known. Factories sprang up all over Louisiana, Cuba, and Mexico, installing and using the "Rillieux System." Later Rillieux also devised a complete blueprint for the drainage of the swamps and lowlands of Louisiana.

In 1881, when he was seventy-five years old, he patented a system of heating juices with vapors in multiple effect which is still used in beet-sugar factories. This patent is said to have reduced fuel consumption by fifty per cent in the French beet-sugar plants which used it.

Norbert Rillieux

Dr. Charles A. Browne, sugar chemist of the U.S. Department of Agriculture, says: "I have held that Rillieux's invention is the greatest in the history of American chemical engineering and I know of no other invention that has brought so great a saving to all branches of chemical engineering."

Today the process of evaporation in multiple effect is universally used throughout the sugar industry as well as in the manufacture of condensed milk, soap, gelatin, and glue, in the recovery of waste liquors in distilleries and paper factories, and in many other processes.

Rillieux worked out a complete sewerage system for the city of New Orleans, but because of his color, he failed to receive the contract. For this reason, and other indignities suffered on account of his color, he decided to return to France.

Scientists, engineers, and technologists have praised Rillieux's important contributions. In 1930, Edward Koppeschaar, a Dutch specialist, with the cooperation of the sugar expert, H. C. Prisen-Geerligs, who was then president of the International Society of Sugar Cane Technologists, started a movement to accord Rillieux the recognition he so richly deserved.

Organizations and scientific societies representing all cane- and beet-sugar countries and territories joined in erecting in the Louisiana State Museum at New Orleans "a bronze memorial to a Negro genius."

The inscription on the tablet reads:

To honor and commemorate
Norbert Rillieux
born at New Orleans, Louisiana, March 18, 1806,
and died at Paris, France, October 8, 1894
Inventor of Multiple Evaporation and its
Application into the Sugar Industry

He died in his eighty-ninth year, and is buried in the Père-LaChaise cemetery in Paris, France.

PETER SALEM

?–1816

Hero of Bunker Hill

Peter salem was born a slave in Framingham, Massachusetts, probably about twenty years before the beginning of the Revolutionary War. Freedom was in the American air, and many slaves in the colonies of England believed that if they fought with the white men for liberty's sake they would be given their freedom. Indeed, the offer of freedom to the slaves drew many into the United States of America.

More than five thousand Negroes, free and slave, fought in the Revolution. Most of them were in the land armies, but many were sailors in the new American navy, the most important ones serving as pilots guiding the vessels among the coastal waters.

One of the earliest battles of the Revolution was

fought on Breed's Hill, a low hill southeast of Bunker Hill, which gave its name to the engagement.

Peter Salem joined the Massachusetts volunteers as a freeman; either he had been freed by his master or had purchased his freedom as many Negroes could in New England. He enlisted under the beloved Continental commander, General Joseph Warren.

We first hear of Peter Salem as fighting at Concord and Lexington, where he was much praised for his endurance and courage. Then he fought with the forces on Breed's Hill. With him were Caesar Bason and Cuffee Whittemore, two other free Negroes. In the other two regiments sent to defend Breed's Hill and Bunker Hill, under William Prescott, were four more Negro freemen, Caleb Howe, Titus Colburn, Alexander Ames, and Basilai Lew.

Although ordered to hold Bunker Hill, Prescott had chosen to fortify a poorer position on Breed's Hill, much lower than Bunker Hill, and more easily flanked from the shores of the Charlestown peninsula.

The Continentals had learned that the British intended to take Charlestown and then move on to the fortifications on Dorchester Heights from which American troops had laid siege to the British in Boston. On June 17, 1775, a hot, bright summer day, General William Howe was ordered to take the position, and moved across the Back Bay from Boston with his warships and men.

Under artillery fire, which ordinarily would have sent such raw, green troops as the Americans into a rout and a retreat, the Continentals continued to stand fast. Peter Salem and the other enlisted men continued their work on the entrenchments with cannonballs whistling over their heads, burying themselves in the earthworks around them. The Continentals were without cannon, and they grumbled to their commander about heat, thirst, and lack of reinforcements, but especially about the lack of cannon to return the British artillery fire.

By midmorning the breastworks of logs and earth, with solid wood platforms, were ready when four small cannon arrived, a pitiful array against the heavy cannon on the British men-of-war, and the field artillery so well maneuvered by the trained regulars. None of the green American officers had been commissioned as they moved into position on Breed's Hill.

The brilliant red coats of the British regulars could be seen with more artillery, pouring into the streets of Boston and down to the waterfront. Howe was bringing over his troops to Charlestown.

Many officers and men skulked away, terrified, but

Prescott let them go, knowing that every ounce of courage would be needed when the British attacked. He did not want cowards in his ranks. Less than a thousand men faced the oncoming British regulars.

Three times the British general ordered the men of the line against the little fortress, and twice such withering fire met them that the hillside was strewn with dead and dying in red coats. On the third assemblage of the forces, as they mounted Breed's Hill under command of Major John Pitcairn, Peter Salem took his place in the gun slot and shot Pitcairn dead. The line wavered and fell back as they carried their commander to the shore.

But the fire from Breed's Hill wavered and failed. Their store of gunpowder was gone. Prescott was forced to order his little band to retreat under cover of the coming night. Although neither side had won a clear victory, the tremendously courageous stand of the small contingent of Continentals raised the morale of the whole country.

A print showing Peter Salem killing the major was run off and sent throughout the colonies, soon to declare themselves free and independent of Great Britain. Peter Salem became the hero of the moment, only second to William Prescott for his courage on that historic day.

Peter Salem continued to serve in other battles for American freedom, and was present at the surrender of General John Burgoyne at Saratoga.

After the Revolutionary War was won, he returned to Framingham, where he died in 1816. In 1882, the town erected a monument over his grave, carved with these words:

> *Peter Salem—Soldier of the Revolution*
> *Died August 16, 1816—Concord*

although he had made his greatest fame, not at Concord and Lexington, where he did fight, but at the Battle of Bunker Hill.

ROBERT SMALLS

1839–1915

Naval Hero

Robert smalls was born to slave parents in 1839 in Beaufort, South Carolina. His parents' owners, unlike many other slaveholders of the time, encouraged their people to learn to read and write. Thus, Robert was able to acquire a little education as he was growing up.

Because Beaufort was so near the sea, the boy came to love ships and sailing. He worked in the dockyards, became a rigger, then a stoker and fireman. He tried to learn all he could about navigation.

Robert Smalls was twenty-three years old when the Civil War broke out. His master hired him out to work as a stevedore on the *Planter*, a 140-foot transport ship that had been converted into an armed frigate by the

Confederate Navy. She could transport 1,400 bales of cotton or 1,000 armed men. The *Planter* was one of the fastest and most valuable ships in Charleston Harbor.

By the time the war started Robert Smalls was already married. He was doing extra work after hours, saving his money in order to buy freedom for himself and his wife and children. His master had agreed that he could do this. Smalls carefully watched every move that the captain and the two mates made, and soon learned to pilot the vessels as well as they. He began to think about getting his wife and children, as well as his brother's family, through the rebel lines to freedom.

His mother, Lydia, had already escaped. She sent word to him by a "contraband" that she had a job as a cook for the Union soldiers. This encouraged him and he set his mind to serious planning.

Smalls noticed that on certain nights the three white officers left the ship and spent the night with their families and friends. He formed a bold plan to round up the families of the Negro crew members, hide them and a few of their belongings on board the *Planter*, and, when all was ready, sail away to freedom. The Negro crew, which included his brother, agreed to the plan. They also agreed that if the plan failed and they were captured, they would either blow up the ship or join hands and jump into the sea, rather than be taken alive.

The night of May 13, 1862, came at last. All was ready: the boilers were fired, the steam up, the mooring ropes cast off, and the anchor hauled aboard. Robert Smalls hoisted the Confederate flag to the highest mast. As they sailed past the fortresses in Charleston Harbor, it appeared to the sentries that the *Planter* was making a night reconnaissance. As they passed each port Smalls, dressed in the captain's uniform and cap, gave the proper signal, and the *Planter* was signaled to proceed.

He breathed much more easily after the *Planter* received the sentry's hail to "Pass the *Planter*" at Fort Sumter, the last of the fortifications. He piloted the ship full steam ahead into the Atlantic. As soon as he was out of sight and range of the rebel shore patrols, he hauled down the Confederate flag and hoisted a white sheet of truce. The *Planter* was soon sighted by a Union gunboat, and, when the two ships met, Robert Smalls turned the *Planter* over to the Union Navy.

For his daring escapade, Smalls received high praise from the Union Navy and prize money for himself and his crew. He was cited in a special report by the Secretary of the Navy to President Lincoln. He was appointed pilot in the Quartermaster's Department of the United States Navy, and took part in an attack on Fort Sumter. Later he was transferred to the *Planter*, with the rank of captain. He remained in the United States Navy for the duration of the Civil War.

When peace came, Robert Smalls became an active politician, and was elected to the Constitutional Convention of South Carolina in 1868. During Reconstruction he was elected to the House of Representatives. He introduced legislation that established free public schools in South Carolina, and instituted many social reforms. He was a fluent speaker, and was respected by the white and Negro people in South Carolina.

After his retirement from politics, Captain Smalls was appointed Collector of the Port of Beaufort. He died in 1915 at the age of seventy-six, his life an inspiration to all Americans who love heroism and daring.

HENRY OSSAWA TANNER

1859–1937

Artist

Henry ossawa tanner was born in Pittsburgh, Pennsylvania, in 1859, the son of a minister in the African Methodist Episcopal church. His father, who was eventually to become a bishop, had plans for Henry's future in the church, and his mother, too, dreamed that her son might some day be a great minister.

But Henry wanted to be a painter. As a boy in Philadelphia he had once seen an artist painting a scene in Fairmont Park. He was fascinated as the artist mixed the dabs of paint and stroked the brush on the canvas to make a picture that came into being in front of his eyes. Henry resolved then and there that he would become an artist.

Henry Ossawa Tanner

He painted his first picture on the back of an old book, redrawing as best he could the picture he had watched the artist paint. In high school, he continued to draw the people and the places he saw every day. He visited the zoo to watch the animals and draw them. He saved his meager allowance for a trip to Atlantic City, so he could paint the ocean.

After he finished high school, he enrolled at the Pennsylvania Academy of Fine Arts, where he could study sculpture as well as painting. His teachers there, among them the famous painter Thomas Eakins, recognized his ability and encouraged him.

After finishing his studies at the Academy, he became a teacher at Clark University in Atlanta, Georgia. He continued to paint, but oils and canvas were expensive and his salary as a college teacher was low, so he became a photographer. He opened a studio near the campus and took pictures in his spare time.

Clark is a Methodist college, and there Tanner met many members of the clergy, some of whom were close family friends. Bishop Daniel A. Payne was a family friend who gave him encouragement and help. He bought several of Tanner's paintings and presented them to Wilberforce University, a Negro church college in Ohio. This encouraged young Tanner to organize a one-man show. He collected his best paintings, and in the fall of 1890 took them to Cincinnati, the nearest large city, where he held his first show. Not one of the pictures was sold, although many people came to the show and admired the work. The exhibition was not a failure, however, because one of the persons who visited it encouraged Tanner to go to Europe to study. So great was his enthusiasm for Tanner's work that he gave the young teacher some of the money for traveling expenses.

With three hundred dollars, Henry Tanner set out for Italy to study the magnificent religious paintings of the world. But on the way he stopped in Paris and there he stayed for a long time. Paris was a painter's city, and Tanner could not bring himself to leave. He sought out great teachers of the city and persuaded them to let him study with them. Benjamin Constant, Jean Léon Gérôme, and Jean Paul Laurens all helped him. Tanner enjoyed the artistic freedom of the city, the warmth of the people of France. In Paris an artist was an artist, regardless of race or color.

So inspired was he by his teachers and his fellow artists that he worked day and night. Paintings streamed from his easel, most of his work depicting religious scenes and people. His strong religious background influenced his choice of subjects. The Bible—its scenes and its characters—was the source of his ideas, and so when he left Paris he went to the Holy Land to study the people and the architecture. After seeing first-hand the shrines, the relics, and the land itself, he returned to Paris, the city he loved, and painted the great religious works for which he was to become famous.

He received official recognition as a painter at the French Salon. In 1897, the French government purchased one of his paintings, *The Resurrection of Lazarus*, to hang in the Luxembourg, one of the greatest art galleries in the world. It hangs there still, admired by thousands of people who visit the gallery every year.

In 1900 he received the Medal of Honor at the Paris Exposition, and in the same year he received the Lippincott Prize in the city in which he had learned to paint. He returned to Philadelphia to accept the award, and brought with him a number of paintings to show to his friends and family. But soon he became homesick for France and its freedoms, so he went back there.

In Paris, his studio had become a meeting place for visitors from all parts of the world. Some of his close friends were the most famous artists of his day. He never again returned to the land of his birth.

Tanner's paintings are easy to understand. They have inspired clergymen and religious workers of all kinds.

Artists have also been inspired by them. His paintings have been bought by galleries all over the world. Some of the most famous are *Christ Walking on the Water, The Disciples on the Road to Bethany, The Destruction of Sodom and Gomorrah,* and *The Flight into Egypt.*

In the Philadelphia Museum of Art in Fairmont Park, near the spot where as a boy Henry Tanner first saw an artist painting, hangs one of his most outstanding pictures, *The Annunciation.* Shortly after it was purchased in 1937, Henry O. Tanner died in Paris, having left a legacy of religious inspiration for the generations to come.

HARRIET TUBMAN

1820–1913

Liberator

ARAMINTA ROSS, who was to become famous under another name, that of Harriet Tubman, was born a slave in Dorchester County, Maryland. She grew up in the slave quarters of her master's plantation, and at six years old was set to work.

Her master had so many slaves that when work on the plantation was slack he sometimes hired the extra ones out to other people. Harriet was sent to a woman who needed a girl to help her with weaving and housework. But her new mistress was impatient and bad-tempered. She soon tired of trying to teach little Harriet how to weave, keep house, and care for the baby, and sent her back to the plantation. This time she went to work in her master's fields. It was a hard life, but she was glad to be back with her parents and older brothers.

As she grew up her family stopped using her pet name of Araminta, and began to call her Harriet, which was also her mother's name. Harriet was hired out only once again, and this time she ran away, back to the plantation and the work on the farm. The slaves worked in the fields from sunup to sundown, and an overseer watched to see that no time was wasted. But there were always whispered conversations, and sometimes a snatch of song in the wind—"Steal away, I ain't got long to stay here." All this was buried deep in Harriet's heart, and she began to dream of freedom.

When her master died, there was a rumor that the plantation and the slaves would be sold. Harriet was a good field hand now, and would bring a high price. She was determined to escape before she was sent south with the chain gang.

Sometime before the master's death Harriet had married a free Negro, John Tubman, but their marriage was not a happy one. When she decided to escape this time she dared not tell her husband, but simply slipped out of their cabin one night. She went straight through the woods to the house of a kind Quaker woman who had once offered to help her. The woman directed Harriet to other "stations" on the Underground Railroad—houses where she found shelter and help on her way north. She was hidden by free Negroes and sympathetic white people in their houses and barns. At night she followed the North Star, and in the daytime she slept in the woods. A farmer drove her part of the way concealed under blankets in his wagon.

Finally she reached Philadelphia, where she found work and freedom. She said later she felt as if she were in heaven: "Everything and everybody looked new!"

As soon as she was settled and rested, she made plans to return and lead others to freedom. She was particularly anxious to get her family away before they were "sold down the river."

During the next months she learned more about the Underground "stations" and the wonderful people who were helping the slaves. This was a dangerous activity for white people, but doubly dangerous for Negroes. Along the routes there were always slave catchers and spies. But hundreds of ways were found to disguise the runaways and hundreds of devices were used to outwit the slave catchers. Harriet soon learned all the cunning traps that were laid, and she had dozens of narrow escapes.

She made nineteen trips back to Maryland, and led bands of slaves numbering in all more than three hundred to freedom. Her most dangerous mission, and her greatest achievement, was the trip when she brought her aged parents out of slavery. She became a legend to the planters and slaves of Maryland. Only the slaves she guided north ever saw her, but many people knew about her. They called her "Moses" because she led her people out of bondage. Her missions were so successful that a reward of $60,000 was offered for the "capture of Harriet Tubman dead or alive." No one was ever able to collect it.

Harriet Tubman worked unceasingly for the cause of freedom. In the course of her work she came to know intimately a number of the abolitionists, such as Frederick Douglass, John Brown, William Seward, and Harriet Beecher Stowe, and she gave many lectures describing her work to antislavery societies in the north.

When the Civil War broke out Harriet served with the Union Army. Governor Andrew of Massachusetts arranged for her to go south aboard a government transport, the *Atlantic*. She worked in an army hospital in Beaufort, on one of the Sea Islands off the coast of South Carolina. There she cared for the sick and homeless slaves who had fled their masters and taken refuge with the Union Army. But more than this, she was an active scout and spy. In 1863 she led a party of Negro soldiers

Harriet Tubman

—former slaves—under Colonel James Montgomery on a raid into enemy country in which nearly eight hundred slaves were freed. An official dispatch said, "She became the only woman in American military history ever to plan and conduct an armed expedition against enemy forces."

After the war she returned to the little house she had bought in Auburn, New York. There she lived with her second husband. She took care of her parents until their deaths, and gave shelter to many homeless and destitute Negroes.

Harriet Tubman lived for nearly a half-century after the Emancipation Proclamation was signed, highly respected and praised throughout the world for her part in helping her people. She died on March 10, 1913. On July 12, 1914, a tablet in her memory was unveiled in Auburn. On it are these words:

> In memory of Harriet Tubman.
> Born a slave in Maryland about 1821.
> Died in Auburn, N.Y., March 10th, 1913.
> Called the Moses of her people,
> During the Civil War. With rare
> Courage she led over three hundred
> Negroes up from slavery to freedom,

And rendered invaluable service
As nurse and spy.
With implicit trust in God
She braved every danger and
Overcame every obstacle. Withal
She possessed extraordinary
Foresight and judgment so that
She truthfully said
"On my Underground Railroad
I nebber run my train off de track
An' I nebber los' a passenger."
This tablet is erected
By the citizens of Auburn.

NAT TURNER

1800–1831

Preacher, Rebel

Nat turner was born into slavery in Southampton County, Virginia, on October 2, 1800. His mother was born in Africa and so hated the idea of bearing a child into slavery that he must have been deeply influenced by her all his life. He himself was an odd, precocious boy, "marked," according to the midwife who attended his mother at his birth, "for great things."

He had a remarkable ability to describe events that had occurred before he was born, and the other slaves were awed by his visions and "voices."

His lot was that of all slave children, though—a hard one. Somehow he managed to learn the alphabet and to teach himself to read the Bible. He became familiar with long passages, which he could recite. He had an inventive mind, and experimented with ways to cast metals and make paper, pottery, and gunpowder.

This steady, serious young man became a Baptist preacher, a fiery speaker with immense religious fanaticism. He lived in a mystical world of his own and claimed to be divinely inspired. He spent much of his time fasting, praying, and reading the Bible, and pondering on the conditions of slavery and the bondage put upon his people. He conversed with the voices he heard, and as he came to greater maturity he developed a greater understanding of himself. He felt he had been destined to free his people.

A confession that he made later when he was tried for insurrection recounts his vision. In May of 1828 a Great Voice spoke to Nat. "Nat Turner, Nat Turner, Nat Turner! Hear me!"

"What is it?" asked Nat.

"The serpent is loosed. The serpent is loosed."

"Yes. Glory!" exclaimed Nat.

"I'm to tell you that Christ has laid down the yoke and that you must take it up again. The time is at hand when the first shall be last and the last shall be first. . . ."

"Thy will be done, Lord," said Nat, and he fell on his knees in prayer.

He had other visions of black and white spirits fighting in the sky. The sun had grown dark and blood gushed down in streams. He saw spots of blood on the earth and blood spattered on the leaves in the woods. He believed that the day of judgment had come for the slaveholders and all their families. The spirit, he believed, would give him a sign to arise and prepare himself and to slay his enemies with their own weapons.

An eclipse of the sun came in February of 1831, and Nat interpreted it as his sign to go forward with his plans. He gathered four disciples, Henry Porter, Hark Travis, Nelson Williams, and Samuel Francis, and "set his face towards Jerusalem." Strangely enough, the county seat of Southampton County was named Jerusalem. He had planned his revolt for July 4, but on that day he was ill. Then another sign appeared in the sky. The sun took on a peculiar color of red on August 13, and Nat set the date of the insurrection for Sunday, August 21.

His four followers gathered in the woods and waited, and during the day, two other slaves joined them. One was an immense fellow named Will, whose face and body were covered with scars from beatings of cruel masters. Nat was later to call him Will the Executioner. When Nat arrived he asked him how he came to be there, and Will said his life was worth no more than others, and his liberty was dear to him.

Nat now outlined his plan to these six men whom he felt he could trust. They would strike that night, going from house to house, killing every white person, even the infants and children. When they had struck terror into their hearts, then they might spare the women and children, for the men would cease to resist.

Although Nat Turner was owned by a man named Putnam Moore, he had been hired out to Joseph Travis on the Travis plantation. It was there, on the night of August 21, that Nat spilled the first blood of that terrible holocaust.

Their only arms were a hatchet and a broadax, which Will handled. They killed Joseph Travis, and his whole family. They took horses and arms and gathered recruits among the slaves. A reign of terror followed, and the records show that fifty-five white persons were killed during the night and the next day.

When they were only three miles from Jerusalem, they were met by about twenty white men armed with guns. Nat ordered his insurrectionists to charge, and the white men fled. As Nat pursued them, he found their forces had been increased by whites from the town, and he had to retreat. He dispersed his men and returned by secret ways to the Travis plantation, where he dug himself a cave and waited for his disciples to rejoin him. They did not come.

By this time soldiers and artillery were sent from Fort Monroe and detachments from warships and hundreds of militiamen from the neighboring states and other Virginia counties. Altogether three thousand armed men were sent to put down the insurrection.

A massacre of Negroes then began, when any slave or freeman even suspected, or simply moving on his own business through the countryside, was shot down without question. No one was ever to know how many hundreds, even thousands, of black men were tortured during questioning and put to death in that terrible time.

Two months passed before Nat Turner gave himself up. He was taken to the county seat in chains, where he pleaded "not guilty," for he said he did not feel guilty. On November 11 he was hanged, and his body given to the surgeons for dissection.

He had prophesied that it would grow dark and rain after he was put to death, and it did rain; then followed a long, dry spell that alarmed both blacks and whites. It was, perhaps, a different kind of dark than Nat Turner had prophesied, for the slaves were more cruelly repressed than before, stricter laws were passed regarding them, and those who feared to free the slaves used this savagery as an argument against freeing them. Those who recognized the immense bravery of the little band and its leader, and believed that whatever man's condition, he will fight to be free, found in Nat Turner's insurrection encouragement and hope for a time when slavery would be ended in America forever.

MAGGIE LENA WALKER

1867–1934

First Woman Bank President

Maggie lena mitchell was born in Richmond, Virginia, on July 15, 1867. Her mother, widowed early, worked hard at the washtub to support her children. Maggie graduated from high school in 1883, when she was not quite sixteen, and became a school teacher. Soon she left the schoolroom to take a course in business administration, her main interest. In 1889, she became executive secretary of the Independent Order of St. Luke. Ten years later she became the organization's secretary-treasurer, and held this position for thirty-five years. In 1890, she married Armstead Walker and, in the course of time, became the mother of two sons.

The original idea behind the Order of St. Luke was

similar to that of many organizations. Each member contributed small weekly dues which would assist him or her to provide for sickness in old age and for funeral expenses. When Mrs. Walker began her work with the organization, she received a salary of only eight dollars a month. For this sum she was expected to collect dues, verify cases of illness and death, keep the books, and pay out all claims.

As the organization grew and the volume of its business expanded, a bank was needed. In 1902, Mrs. Walker brought a plan for the St. Luke Penny Savings Bank before the council of the order. Although the bank was to bear the name of the order, it was to be legally separate. She persuaded the council to adopt her plan, and became president of the new enterprise. She learned the business from the ground up. The institution became the St. Luke Bank and Trust Company, numbering among its accounts those of Richmond's city tax, gas, and water departments.

Mrs. Walker's influence continued to widen. She became president of the state branch of the National Association of Colored Women, and served on numerous other boards and councils. All the while she was planning a great future for her bank. She wanted to have both the Order of St. Luke and the bank on such a firm

Maggie Lena Walker

basis that they could continue to move steadily forward when she was gone.

She succeeded admirably, and was the first woman to be the founder and president of a bank in the United States.

BOOKER TALIAFERRO WASHINGTON

About 1858–1915

Educator, Humanitarian

BOOKER TALIAFERRO WASHINGTON was born near Hale's Ford, Franklin City, Virginia, about 1858. Not being certain of the exact date of his birth, he chose to celebrate it on Easter Sunday, whenever it might fall. His mother was an intelligent slave woman. He never knew his father, who was white.

After Emancipation the boy and his family went to Malden, Virginia. As a youth he had to work in a salt furnace to help support the family. He was so anxious for an education that he began to teach himself, and made such progress that, at the age of fourteen, he was ready to enter Hampton Institute. He started out with very little money and walked practically the whole five hundred miles from his home to the school.

Washington worked his way through the Institute as a janitor, and in a few years was graduated with high standing. Shortly after his graduation he was recommended by General Armstrong of Hampton as the best possible choice to head a normal school for rural Negroes in a small Alabama village. With a meager salary, a leaky building, and himself as the only teacher, Booker T. Washington founded the now world-famous Tuskegee Institute.

His philosophy was based on the "Three H's": Head, Heart, and Hand. Tuskegee graduates became prominent in many fields, and Tuskegee's president was recognized as one of the outstanding Negro leaders of his day, beloved and respected by all Americans. Presidents of the United States sought his advice on problems relating to the Negro. He received many honorary degrees from colleges and universities, among them Harvard and Dartmouth.

He died prematurely at the age of fifty-seven from overwork, and is buried on the campus of the school which he founded. A beautiful monument to his memory also stands there, but it is in his inspiring example that his greatest memorial may be found.

PHILLIS WHEATLEY

About 1753–1784

First Poet of Her People

A LITTLE SLAVE GIRL on the auction block in Boston about the year 1761 attracted the sympathy of John Wheatley, a well-to-do tailor. He bought the child and took her to his home, where she was treated with kindness and given the family name.

She was given a room of her own, and taught to read the Bible and write. Soon she began to make up rhymes and, at the age of fourteen, she was writing poetry— serious poetry. The Wheatleys encouraged her, and took pride in her writing. Sometimes she wrote about a friend who had died, sometimes she wrote about events of the day.

When war broke out in the colonies, Phillis wrote a poem about George Washington and, at the suggestion of Mr. Wheatley, sent it to the General. He sent her a gracious letter thanking her for her thoughts. He closed by saying, "If you should ever come to Cambridge or near Headquarters, I shall be happy to see a person so favored by the muses, and to whom nature has been so liberal and beneficent in her dispensations. I am with great respect your Obedient Humble Servant, George Washington."

In 1773 the Wheatleys sent Phillis, who had been freed, on a trip to London. There she was a guest of the Countess of Huntingdon. The Lord Mayor presented her with a beautiful edition of John Milton's *Paradise Lost*. She was invited to the Court to be presented to the King, and was feted everywhere.

Suddenly word came that Mrs. Wheatley, the only mother she had ever known, was gravely ill. Phillis sailed for home, just in time to see her beloved mistress before she died.

While she was in England, friends of the Wheatleys had suggested that Phillis's poems be published. In 1773, after her return to Boston, her first book, *Poems on Various Subjects, Religious and Moral*, was issued in a small edition. As soon as the book came out, many persons expressed doubt that the author was a Negro. But the governor of Massachusetts and seventeen other leading citizens wrote a letter to the newspapers assuring the public that the poems were indeed written by Phillis Wheatley, who had once been a slave.

Five years after the death of Mrs. Wheatley, Phillis married a man named John Peters. Their life was not happy. John Peters was a failure in business, and after a few years he left Phillis with three small children to care for. The dire poverty in which she lived resulted in the death of two of her children. Phillis herself became ill in the winter of 1784, and died on December 5 of that year. Her youngest child died the same day, and they were buried together.

But through her days of hardship and sorrow she had continued to write, and a few days after her death one of her finest poems was published. It was inspired by the end of the Revolutionary War: *Liberty and Peace*, a fitting conclusion to the rich and creative life she had led.

"BERT" WILLIAMS

1876–1922

Comedian, Actor

Egbert Austin Williams was born on the island of New Providence in the Bahamas in 1876. When Bert was only two years old, his parents brought him to New York City, but they later moved to Riverside, California. There the boy grew up and graduated from high school. At first he studied civil engineering in San Francisco, but soon his interest turned to the theater.

His first theatrical engagement was with a mountebank minstrel company that played in the mining and lumber camps of California and Oregon. In 1895, Williams took as his partner George Walker, a vaudeville showman, and the two appeared as a team on the very popular vaudeville stage of that day.

The Williams and Walker team became famous, appearing in New York in 1896 at Tony Pastor's and in 1897 at Koster and Bial's theaters. In 1900 they opened in *The Song of Ham*, a musical farce that ran for two years. In this show, Williams played the part of a burnt-cork comic and Walker that of a high-style, well-dressed dandy. Their greatest success, *In Dahomey*, opened in 1902. Based on a book by Jess A. Ships, with music by Will Marion Cook and lyrics by Paul Laurence Dunbar, the farce was so popular that they took it to London. There they played a command performance at Buckingham Palace for King Edward VII.

Williams and Walker headed their own production company, which brought such plays as *The Policy Players*, *Bandanna Land*, and *Abyssinia*, to the theatrical circuit. *Abyssinia* set a record for its time by running ten weeks on Broadway.

After Walker died in 1909, Williams became a featured performer in all-white Broadway musicals. In 1910 he signed a long-term contract with the Ziegfeld Follies, and he toured American cities with them for ten years in many editions of that review. His best known singing and recording numbers from these shows were his own *Nobody*, Irving Berlin's *Woodman Spare That Tree*, and Will Cook's *O Death, Where Is Thy Sting*.

He always sang in a mournful bass voice and represented himself as a lazy, good-for-nothing fellow, a part that he initiated. It was later much imitated, most notably by the radio comedians who produced Amos 'n' Andy, and by Eddie Cantor on the stage.

Present-day comedians avoid poking fun at any race by overemphasis on conventional notions about them, by using dialect or other racial characteristics. The amusing characterizations by Red Skelton and similar comedians stem directly, however, from the successful creations of Bert Williams.

Bert Williams was not merely a comedian, but also a serious student whose interests covered many areas. He was familiar with the works of Voltaire, Tom Paine, Goethe, Plato, and Schopenhauer, and his mastery of the art of pantomime and monologue styles has never been surpassed by any other comedian on the American stage, Negro or white.

Eddie Cantor, a friend of the comedian, said of him, "As a performer, he was close to genius. As a man, he was everything the rest of us would like to have been. As a friend, he was without envy or jealousy."

The March 11, 1922, issue of *Billboard*, an actors' and showmen's newspaper, stated: "E. A. Williams, known to the theatrical world as 'Bert' Williams, and regarded by many as the greatest comedian on the American stage, died at his home March 4, of pneumonia. He collapsed on the stage in Detroit, Monday, February 7, while appearing in *Under the Bamboo Tree*, and was taken to New York, Thursday, when it was found he was suffering from pneumonia. Blood transfusion was ordered, but Williams failed to react."

So passed one of the best loved figures of the American stage and the first American of African descent to make an important success in the American theater. He led the way for others like Bill Robinson, Eddie Anderson, who plays "Rochester" in the Jack Benny shows, and Dick Gregory, who, like Bert Williams, writes his own unique satire, which points up as it mocks the wrongs that need righting across the land.

DANIEL HALE WILLIAMS

1858–1931

Surgeon

D ANIEL HALE WILLIAMS, pioneer surgeon called the "Father of Negro Hospitals," was born in Hollidaysburg, Pennsylvania, January 18, 1858. After the death of his father, he was taken to live with relatives in Janesville, Wisconsin. As a small boy he enjoyed reading, which led him to explore the fields of science and medicine.

During his elementary- and high-school years he worked at many odd jobs. One of his employers, Mr. Charles Anderson, took an interest in him and persuaded Henry Palmer, the Surgeon-General of Janesville, to let the boy study medicine in his office.

After two years of study, Williams passed the entrance examination at the Chicago Medical College, which later became Northwestern University School of Medicine. He was graduated from Northwestern in 1883, and interned at Mercy Hospital, a Catholic institution in Chicago. After graduation he was invited to become an instructor of anatomy at Northwestern.

At the time Dr. Williams graduated there were no training schools for Negro nurses and few hospitals where young Negro doctors were permitted to train as internes. So Dr. Williams called a meeting of interested citizens, both Negro and white, and together they founded Provident Hospital and Training School for Nurses, which opened its doors in 1891.

In 1893 President Grover Cleveland called Daniel Williams to Washington, D.C., and offered him the position of Surgeon-General of Freedmen's Hospital, a government hospital. After five years in that post he returned to Chicago, where he served with the Cook County Hospital and was on the staff of St. Luke's Hospital from 1907 to 1931, the first Negro doctor to operate there.

Dr. Williams is most famous for his successful operation on the human heart. On July 10, 1893, he performed the operation which was to immortalize his name—the first successful suture of the human heart on

Daniel Hale Williams

record. This operation was performed at his beloved Provident Hospital in Chicago.

He was one of the founders of the National Medical Association, and a charter member of the American College of Surgeons. He taught surgery at Meharry Medical College in Nashville, Tennessee, during many of its summer clinics. He also served as a member of the Chicago Board of Health from 1887 to 1889. He spent much time traveling and lecturing in order to help build hospitals and training schools for Negroes in many cities, such as Atlanta, Dallas, Nashville, and Louisville. He died in 1931.

CARTER GOODWIN WOODSON

1875–1950

Scholar, Historian

C ARTER G. WOODSON was born on December 19, 1875, at New Canton, Virginia. He came from a large family, and was not able to attend the district school during much of its five-month term because his parents, who were newly freed slaves, needed him to work on the farm.

By serious application to his studies, however, he mastered the fundamentals of common school subjects. Then, ambitious for more education, he and his brother moved to Huntington, West Virginia, where they hoped to attend Douglass High School. But even here he had to work in the coal mines and could attend school only a few months of the year.

In 1895, when he was twenty years old, he at last entered high school, and two years later he was graduated with honors. After another two years of study at Berea College in Kentucky, he began teaching school, and he was soon able to return to Douglass High School —as its principal.

He continued his studies at Berea during the summer vacations until he became a supervisor of schools in the Philippine Islands. During his four years in the Philippines, he learned to speak fluent Spanish. On his return to the United States he continued his studies at the University of Chicago, where he received his Bachelor of Arts degree in 1907, and a Master of Arts degree in 1908.

He then spent a year abroad, doing graduate work in history at the Sorbonne in Paris and perfecting his French. In 1909, he became a high-school teacher in Washington, D.C., and was able to carry on research in the Library of Congress for his dissertation, "The Disruption of Virginia," which earned him the degree of Doctor of Philosophy at Harvard in 1912.

During all these years, Carter Woodson was reading and doing research on the Negroes in America and Africa. He was convinced that if a race had no recorded history, its achievements would be forgotten and, in time, claimed by other groups. He found that many of the achievements of Negroes were overlooked, ignored, and even suppressed by writers of history textbooks and by the teachers who used them. Woodson's one ambition was that Negro youth should grow up with a firm knowledge of the contributions of the Negro to American history. Indeed, his entire life was devoted to this cause. "Race prejudice," said Dr. Woodson, "grows naturally from the idea that the Negro race is inferior."

Though often ridiculed for his aim, Dr. Woodson persisted, and, bit by bit, he gathered and sorted information. His monumental record of the lost and ignored history of the American Negro became the basis for a number of books on the subject. Another outgrowth of his studies was the founding of the Association for the Study of Negro Life and History, which held its first meeting in Chicago, Illinois, in 1915. The Association now has its permanent headquarters in Washington, D.C.

The following year saw the publication of the *Journal of Negro History*, a scientific quarterly which is published by the Association for the Study of Negro Life and History.

Dr. Woodson continued to teach. He was Dean of the School of Liberal Arts at Howard University, then

Dean of West Virginia State College. During this period he published *The Negro in Our History*, a college textbook which has been used and quoted widely throughout the United States.

He followed his book with publication of the *Negro History Bulletin*, which is a magazine issued during the school year for use in elementary and high schools. The *Bulletin* is also published by the Association for the Study of Negro Life and History. In 1926, he established Negro History Week, which is celebrated each year in February, at a period which covers the birthdates of both Abraham Lincoln and Frederick Douglass.

During his lifetime, Dr. Woodson was the recipient of many honors, among them the Spingarn Medal, which he received in 1926 for "outstanding achievement in the field of Research and History of the Negro," and an honorary doctorate for his work on the history of the Negro from Virginia State College in 1941.

He died on April 3, 1950. Shortly thereafter, a high school in Washington, D.C., was named for him. But his name will live longest through his books and his pioneer researches into the history of his race.

CHARLES YOUNG

1864–1922

Army Officer

NEGROES HAVE FOUGHT valiantly in all of our country's wars. They have been honored veterans of the Revolutionary War, the War of 1812, the Civil War, the Spanish-American War, World War I, World War II, and, most recently, the Korean action.

Charles Young was a Negro who saw action in the Spanish-American War and rose to the highest rank of any Negro of his time. The future colonel was born March 12, 1864, in Mayslick, Kentucky. His parents moved to Ohio where he finished his education and became a school teacher. In 1884, he received an appointment to the United States Military Academy at West Point, the ninth Negro to be admitted. The prejudiced southern cadets tried to discourage the young Negro by heaping every kind of insult upon him, but

Young performed his duties faithfully, ignored the insults, and was graduated in 1889. He was commissioned as a second lieutenant in the all-Negro Tenth Cavalry.

In 1894, Young taught military science at Wilberforce University. When the Spanish-American War broke out in 1898 he was promoted to the rank of major, put in charge of the Ninth Ohio Regiment, and sent to Cuba. Even though they suffered gross discrimination, the Ninth and Tenth Cavalries distinguished themselves at San Juan Hill when they came to the aid of Teddy Roosevelt and his Rough Riders. One of the white corporals stated: "If it had not been for the Negro cavalry, the Rough Riders would have been exterminated." Some believed that the strength of the Negro troops turned the tide of battle and won the Spanish fort.

Young later held commissions in the Philippine Islands and in Haiti. In 1915, after seeing action with a squadron of the Tenth Cavalry against the Mexican guerillas, he was made a lieutenant colonel and led further raids against Pancho Villa.

Despite his outstanding record of bravery, his military knowledge, and his rank and experience, Young was not assigned to European service in World War I because of racial prejudice. To prove that he was in top physical condition, he rode a horse from Xenia, Ohio, to Washington and back again, but still he was not permitted to fight for his country.

Five days before the Armistice was signed, Colonel Young received orders to report to Camp Grant in Illinois, where he was to be in charge of trainees. He was later sent to Monrovia, Liberia, as a military attaché to help reorganize the Liberian army. This pleased him because it gave him a chance to deepen his interest in African life and culture.

Unlike most military men, Young had an interest in literature and music, played piano and cornet, and spoke Spanish, French, and German. He was a popular speaker, and the Negro people were proud of him. While in Lagos, Nigeria, Young fell ill and died in 1922. He was buried in the National Cemetery at Arlington, Virginia, with full military honors. A tall marble shaft marks his resting place.

INDEX

Abbott, Robert S., 1–5
abolitionists, 44–45, 49–51, 71, 80–81, 129
Abolitionist Society, 50
Abyssinia, 147
Accra, Ghana, 58
actors, 6–11, 146–149
Africa, 43–45, 57–58, 159
African Free School, 6
African Methodist Episcopal Church, 13–16, 36, 75
"African Theatre" ("Brown's"), 8
agricultural research, 40–42
Aldridge, Amanda Ira, 11
Aldridge, Amanda Paulina, 11
Aldridge, Daniel, 6–7
Aldridge, Ira Frederick, 6–11
Aldridge, Margaret, 10–11
Allen, Richard, 12–16
American College of Surgeons, 152
American Missionary Society, 45
American Negro Academy, 73–74
American Red Cross, 54
American Revolution, *see* Revolutionary War

American Social Science Association, 74
Ames, Alexander, 113
Amherst College, 53
Amistad, 43–44
Anderson, Charles, 150
Anderson, Eddie, 149
Anderson, Hans Christian, 10
Andrews, Charles, 6–7
Andrews, Charles C., 70
Annunciation, The, 125
Anti-Slavery Society, 81
Arlington National Cemetery, 159
artists, 91–92, 121–125
Ashley, Henry, 28–29
Association for the Study of Negro Life and History, 155, 156
astronomer, 20–23
Atlanta University, 56, 62, 88
Attucks, Crispus, 17–19
Auburn, N.Y., 130–131
Auld family, 47, 51
authors, 52, 55–58, 59–62, 72–74, 80–82, 88–90, 143–145, 155–156

160

Index

Index

Index

ABOUT THE AUTHOR

Charlemae Hill Rollins was born in Yazoo City, Mississippi. She studied at Western University, Columbia University, and the University of Chicago.

Mrs. Rollins has been active in education and library work for many years. She taught children's literature, was a children's librarian at the Chicago Public Library, has written articles for many publications, and has edited several anthologies. She has also lectured extensively in the United States and has visited libraries in London, Paris, Rome, Stockholm, and Oslo.

Among the numerous awards she has received are The American Brotherhood Award and the Distinguished Service Award of the Children's Reading Round Table. In 1962, she made the presentation of the Jane Addams Children's Book Award in the Nobel Peace Institute in Oslo, Norway.

She lives with her husband in Chicago, Illinois. They have one son.